Hell's Geek

By
Eve Langlais

(Welcome to Hell #5)

Disclaimer and Copyright

Published by Eve Langlais
1606 Main Street
PO Box 151
Stittsville, ON
Canada
K2S1A3
www.EveLanglais.com

ISBN-13: 978-1517245481
ISBN-10: 1517245486

Chapter One

"Whatever happens, no matter what, don't lose the oar." The first rule in the ferryman's handbook.

The river monster rose from the deep, a massive leviathan with only one evil purpose.

To steal his damned oar.

Adexios held it tight, determined to win. Alas, this time went the same as past tug of wars. The long wooden pole, with its wide paddle end, was torn from Adexios' grasp. Third time this week.

Charon, the river master, would freak. Dear old dad thought Adexios lost his paddles on purpose. It wasn't Adexios' fault the Styx monsters were working against him.

"Are you fucking kidding me?" he yelled at the gigantic beast with its massive hump.

Rather than diving back down, it remained to taunt him as it happily munched the oar while eyeballing Adexios with giant, lidless orbs.

"Don't you give me pretty eyes," he snarled. "This is not funny. Now how the hell am I supposed to ferry this newest crew to Hades Port?"

Hades Port, a massive wharf in the third ring, serviced new arrivals. It never closed and always had some of Lucifer's staff on hand, ready to usher damned souls to their newest lot in un-life. If a person was only moderately bad, they paid a small penance then got to eke out an existence in one of the many rings. Those who were truly evil got the star treatment and their screams rang on the hour and could be counted on to set the time on clocks.

Turning to the quiet crowd, he eyed them where they sat huddled in the middle of the flat-bottomed boat. Some of them still wore a dazed look, unable to comprehend the fact that they'd earned the pit and not entrance to heaven—which had ridiculously impossible high standards.

Adexios cleared his throat. "So, um, we've kind of run into a problem. That was my only oar." Actually it was his spare, as his original one had also been munched. "We need to get this boat moving. Any volunteers to get in the water and pull us across the river?"

As a group, the damned souls glanced to the monster still lounging alongside and, of course, it chose that moment to smile, showing jagged teeth with fleshy bits caught between. The souls snuggled closer together and shook their heads violently.

Adexios sighed. *Looks like I'm getting wet again.* But at least this time he'd brought a swimsuit.

The last time he'd had to go for a dip was the day he'd worn jeans under his robe, and in a sadistic twist of fate, he'd not worn underwear for some reason. While he wasn't against skinny-dipping per se, he didn't like exposing himself, especially to strangers.

Another point against naked dips? The tentacles that felt a need to taunt his more delicate manparts as he scissor-kicked behind the boat. After that last time, he'd thought his balls would never come out of hiding, and even remembering the slimy touch still made them shrink.

With a heavy sigh, he changed into his swim gear, ignoring the snickered, "Look at how white his butt is."

Try getting a tan when the sun never technically

shone. Hiking his shorts over said pale butt, Adexios eyed the dark water. Murky and not the most pleasant smelling, at least it wasn't cold this far into the rings. The lower section that joined with the Darkling Sea on the other hand… Brrr, chilly.

Adexios had no sooner slipped into the water than a tentacle came slyly exploring. Reaching under the water, he grasped it and gave it a twist.

"Not today. I've got a job to do. And I'm late as it is."

Hours later, his legs not as sore as expected—how could they be when he swam so many times a bloody week?—Adexios tugged his boat to its assigned dock, all his passengers accounted for, albeit slightly traumatized by his lily white legs.

Gripping the ladder, he began to climb, only to stop as his head came even with the weathered boards and he caught sight of the hem belonging to a familiar black robe.

"Oh, hi, Dad."

Charon moved back a pace, or more like drifted, having perfected the art of eerie movement centuries ago. Speculation abounded as to what hid under his dad's robes. Even Adexios wasn't quite sure. Dad never took them off, and Adexios' mother never told.

"Don't you hi dad me. How in all that's evil did you lose another freaking oar?"

"A sea monster ate it."

"That answer didn't wash when you were a kid practicing your paddling, and it doesn't wash now. I understand you're trying to curtail Lucifer's favor by lying, but I am your father," Charon boomed, "and I won't have it."

Except Adexios wasn't lying. The damned sea monsters had eaten his oar, and his Brussels sprouts. But that was a secret he gladly kept to himself. "Whatever, Dad. I lost it, okay? On purpose. Happy now?"

A grunt was his father's eloquent reply.

"Can I go home and grab a shower now if you're done reaming me out?" The Styx wasn't the cleanest river to swim in.

"You don't have time. Lucifer wants to see you."

Great. Could this day get any worse? Being sought out by the big man of Hell himself was never a good thing, especially not given the numerous mishaps that kept happening to him. Such as a little while back when he had that mutiny on board his boat of souls.

Again, not my fault.

His dad thought he was napping on the job when the damned ones hijacked his ferry and dumped Adexios on an island. Being knocked unconscious apparently didn't work as an excuse. Nor did it make him eligible for worker's compensation, or so he found out after he filled out forms Hell-AC one through one hundred and thirteen, with appendices A through BY. Damned paper pushers. They liked to torture even those who didn't deserve punishment.

"I need a shower before I go anywhere." And some clothes. Hedonism might be poplar in Hell, but Adexios preferred to keep his body covered. Especially since his tall, lanky frame didn't fare as well in the bulky muscle department compared to the demons that bench-pressed boulders with prisoners strapped on them just for fun.

"Are you intentionally defying me and Lucifer?"

No, he just wanted a damned shower.

"Ass-kissing has a time and place, son," his father lectured.

"Whatever," he muttered as he leaned over to grab his robe from the boat. His father was still talking as

Adexios left, shoes in hand, his wet feet clomping the dock boards putting to rest rumors, in his case at least, that he'd inherited his father's mysterious physique.

As he made it the few blocks from the wharf to his apartment over a bar, he pondered what Lucifer could possibly want. Reaming him out in person was a possibility. Commending him on breaking the rules, even if by accident, also a potential outcome. Or perhaps, Lucifer, in his quest to rebuild his minion army, had turned his sights Adexios' way.

I hope not.

It was no longer a secret that the Lord of Darkness was playing matchmaker, and while he seemed to have had some success, the devil also had some failures that were buried, literally, in the dune deserts of Hell in the eighth ring.

Surely the big guy had other minions to torture, bigger, stronger ones. Adexios, while fit, certainly wasn't the strongest, not by a long shot. Nor was he superbly dexterous or imbued of magic, unless what-the-fuckery counted. His only claim to fame, other than being related to his dad, was being clumsy and book smart. But intelligence was vastly underrated in Hell.

Adexios, to his parents' shame, had been a straight-A student, and a genius when it came to math. When the other demons' mothers proudly boasted that their child was barely passing in school, his poor mother had to hang her head in mortification as he achieved honors.

Despite the punishments—no fresh fruit, no reading allowed, and being kept awake past his bedtime—he couldn't help himself. Knowledge just stuck to him, kind of like the river gunk.

Stripping, he dumped his clothes in the garbage chute that, through some kind of weird magic, ended up in the furnace of Hell. Fuel to feed the fire.

Standing under the hot spray of his shower, he'd just soaped himself when a deep voice said, "Tell me you're whacking off and not actually bathing to avoid your meeting with me."

Hear that unmanly squeak? Yeah, that came from him as he clung to the curtain and peeked around the edge. "What are you doing in my bathroom?"

Lucifer's dark brows arched. "I left strict instructions that I wanted to meet with you the moment you brought in your boat—late again. While I commend you on never being on time, especially since it drives my staff nuts, defying me isn't conducive to a long and torture-free life. Some would even say it's moronic."

"Really?" Adexios brightened. "I don't suppose you could tell my mom I did something stupid? It would totally make her day."

You'd think that a grown man in his thirties wouldn't give a shit anymore, but when his mom was happy, she baked, and given his cooking skills equaled varying degrees of burnt, he could use some home-cooking lest he wither to skin and bones. He was, after all, his father's son.

"Mama's boy," Lucifer uttered with a shake of his head.

The devil said it as if it was a bad thing. Adexios had two-dozen homemade oatmeal raisin confections in his Cookie Monster jar that said otherwise.

"Is there any particular reason you felt a need to rush our meeting? I was planning to come as soon as I washed and put on some clean clothes."

"So finish off and get dressed. We need to talk." Lucifer hopped onto the vanity and crossed his arms, whistling as he waited.

"Um, could you like maybe step into the next

room while I finish?"

"Feeling inadequate?" Lucifer smirked. "I can't really blame you. My wench doesn't call me her stallion for nothing."

"I thought it was because your fear of commitment made you run like the wind."

The devil's eyebrows drew together in a large black hairy beetle. "I fear nothing. Not even our upcoming"—Lucifer swallowed hard—"engagement party. The horror of it. Whatever happened to living in sin? I like sin. I encourage sin. But oh no, she wants to get married she says. She wants to lock me into a monogamous agreement. It's utterly unnatural."

Given Lucifer's woebegone look, Adexios couldn't help but throw him a verbal helping hand. "But just think of the benefits. Now when you stay late after work, and she harangues you, you can accuse her of stifling you, of not trusting, and of not wanting you to get ahead with your work."

"You mean start a fight?" Lucifer perked up. "Fighting means makeup sex. I excel at makeup sex. And spontaneous sex. And…"

As Lucifer went on to list the many ways he excelled at fornication, Adexios popped his head back in the shower. Rinsing off the rest of the soap, he wondered, with a curiosity that plagued the mentally acute, what had brought Lucifer to his home.

Locks couldn't keep the devil out if he wanted to see a person. The big guy had the ability to pop in on anyone anywhere in Hell, but he didn't do it often. Lucifer claimed a trick like that was most effective when used sparingly. Apparently, the screams were more authentic that way.

Clean at last, Adexios shut off the water then grimaced. Whoever had built this place hadn't been thinking when they put the towel bar out of reach of the shower. This meant he'd have to flash his boss. No big deal. After all, Lucifer truly had seen it all.

And I've nothing to be ashamed of.

Adexios yanked the plastic curtain to the side and stepped out. However, his hand froze in the process of reaching for a towel as he noted, while Lucifer sat atop his vanity, still expositing on the virtues of his lovemaking, a tall, very tall, woman stood in his bathroom.

Did he mention she was very attractive too? Blonde hair swept into a high ponytail, a muscular body that retained an hourglass shape displayed in a warrior-woman outfit consisting of a leather corset, which pushed her breasts high and created a shadowy valley, tight leather shorts hugging curvy hips meant for grabbing, and knee-high black boots that were just fucking hot. She also wore a sword at her side and a very amused expression.

"Well, hello there," she said, her voice husky and sensual.

Too sensual. A certain part of him perked in interest, and Adexios fervently wished, as his cheeks heated, that a Styx monster would rise from the shower drain and swallow him whole.

Chapter Two

"If you don't plan to screw it, then kill it."
Amazon rule coined by The Black Widow.

He's blushing.

Surely a first in Hell, and definitely a first for Valaska. Most men would have preened at getting caught slick and naked by her. Amazon women were known to be voracious and lusty lovers.

Given their reputation, the boner the naked guy sported was not surprising in the least. What did manage to shock her was his yelled, "There's a woman in my bathroom!" He then popped back into the shower and hid behind the curtain.

Seriously?

She glanced over at Lucifer, who shrugged. "The boy is modest. Not sure how that happened, what with him being raised in the pit."

Modesty in Hell. The idea was practically laughable. The pit was a place where inhibitions were waived and hedonistic views prevailed. Nudity did not carry any stigma. Down here, it was clothing required beaches that were in the minority.

"Is he going to hide in there all day?"

"*He,*" said the guy in the shower, "would like a little privacy to get dressed. So could you please get out?"

"Please?" Lucifer grimaced. "Did you seriously just say that to gross me out?"

Naked man peeked around the curtain, brows

knit in a frown. He opened his mouth to speak, but instead of words, he yelped, probably because he suddenly lost his footing and scrabbled to hold on to the curtain, which ripped, the tinkling sound of the rings being shaken loose almost musical. Less harmonic was the thump as the guy hit the bottom of the tub, wrapped in plastic, groaning.

"Um, are you all right?" she asked.

"Uhn."

"Is that a yes or a no?"

A steady handclap from Lucifer stole her attention. "On a clumsy scale of one to ten, I rate that a solid eight point three," Lucifer announced.

Another groan emerged from the shower curtain heap in the tub. "You are not funny. I need to get dressed, so if you don't mind, would you get out of my bathroom?"

"What if I do mind?"

"Get the fuck out!" shouted the man, who'd finally lost all patience.

"That's better. About time you stopped being so bloody polite." Lucifer slid off the vanity and stalked back into the main living area, which didn't boast much in ways of décor or furniture, unless the stacks of books counted.

Following the devil, Valaska took notes of some of the titles, *The First Six Books of the Elements of Euclid* by John Casey and *The Evanston Colloquium: Lectures on Mathematics* by Felix Klein.

Sounded dry and boring, but the paperback peeking from under a sofa cushion, *Kodiak's Claim*, proved an interesting title, especially given the cover featured a bare-chested man and a bear. What an odd choice of reading material for the repressed man in the bathroom. A man she found surprisingly attractive—if a tad skinny.

While not a giant by any means, he at least matched her in height, which put him over six feet. His shoulders were wide, and he didn't appear to bear an ounce of fat, but neither was he a man who worked out six hours a day or took bulking supplements. His physique was lean, very lean, which made the length and width of his cock jarring.

I don't know why he's so shy about showing it off. He definitely had reason to boast, and yes, she took notice. As a woman of lusty appetite, Valaska wasn't shy when it came to choosing bed partners.

Perching herself on a barstool in front of the small countertop for his kitchen—an area that bore scorch marks on the ceiling and cupboards as well as the lingering smell of smoke—she leaned her elbows back and perused the man she currently worked for.

Lucifer. Lord of the pit himself. Appearing in his forties, he was currently attired in a suit, a black pin-striped affair with a light pink shirt and a tie that bore— she leaned forward just to be sure—fuchsia-colored flamingoes.

"Nice tie," she remarked.

"I know. I have a tailor who handcrafts all my outfits and oversees the creation of wonderful accents such as this tie."

"But what's up with the footwear?"

Lucifer peered down at his bright red duckie slippers, sporting an ivory set of horns. "Dammit. I meant to change out of those before coming to this meeting."

"They look…comfortable."

"They are. Gaia hates them though. Says the duckies give her the willies. She banned my matching onesie from our bedroom."

"The horror." And she didn't mean Gaia's decision but more the fact that the lord of the pit wore a onesie.

"Not even married yet and already she's dictating to me. Which reminds me, I need to dick-tate to her later." Lucifer winked.

Valaska knew better than to reply to his innuendo. There was nothing worse than getting caught by Lucifer when he launched into one of his boastful speeches about his abilities as a lover. Especially since he was off the market so no one could demand he prove his skill.

Speaking of skill, apparently hers were required. Lucifer had requested a capable warrior and since the Amazonian Queen, Thora, owed the guy a favor, and Valaska had lost the arm wrestling match, she now found herself in his employ, but she still had yet to fully grasp in what capacity.

"So what's up with the prima donna in the bathroom?" Valaska asked, and why had the devil insisted she accompany him to meet the guy? It wasn't as if Mr. RedCheeks-BigDick posed a threat.

"Adexios is *special*."

She didn't miss the inflection. "Hockey helmet special?"

"Not quite."

"Germaphobe special?"

"Possibly."

"Going to achieve great things kind of special?" She threw that out there, even if she didn't quite believe it.

"Very great things. You both are actually going to achieve wondrous things."

Why did she not trust the smile on Lucifer's lips and the calculating gleam in his eye?

"What he means to say," the no-longer-naked guy said exiting the bathroom, "is he's got some kind of twisted plot, and he's decided we're going to play in it."

"Twisted? I like that." The devil preened as if given the highest compliment.

"Is he telling the truth? Are you planning to use us in some devious scenario?"

"While I usually try to avoid the T word, in this case"—Lucifer beamed—"indeed I am planning to use you to further my greatness. You're welcome by the way."

"Will it involve violence?" she asked, going straight for the important part.

"I should hope so," Satan answered.

"Awesome. I'm in."

"You're in?" the guy sputtered. "But you don't even know what you're agreeing to?"

She shrugged. "As long as I get to kill things or smack them around, I'm good. Beats doing beach patrol back home." Amazons had very simple goals in life. Eat, sleep, fight, and die with glory in battle.

"Aren't you just the most agreeable girl." Lucifer grimaced. "I'll allow it in this instance, but for future reference, I do expect a little bit of back talk. How else am I supposed to keep my dire glare in fine form? Do you think the art of intimidation comes easily? Well, it does for me, but still, a demon should practice it, lest he get rusty."

"Well, you can practice it on me," announced the fellow, who'd dressed in, of all things, a pale blue button-down shirt and beige khakis. Add in a pencil protector and glasses and he'd totally rock the nerd look. "I don't do violence. It's bad enough I've got to deal with those Styx monsters constantly trying to make me look incompetent. I don't need some steroid-using demon beating the crap out of me to make myself feel good."

"Perhaps if you didn't let them beat you up, you wouldn't feel so bad," she advised.

He didn't like her suggestion and shot her a glare. "Who are you anyhow, and why are you here?"

Lucifer clapped his hands and rubbed them together. "Ah, yes, did I forget to make introductions. Adexios, son of Charon, current occupation boatman in charge of ferrying the souls, meet Valaska, Amazon ass-kicking bitch."

She puffed out her chest—which was quite impressive in her current corset, something both Lucifer and Adexios noticed. A compliment from the big man was a thing to take pride in. And, yes, that meant brownie points, as pride was one of the basic sins. If she kept this up, she might even earn a bonus on this job.

"And why is an Amazon warrior in my living room?" Adexios asked.

"Because she's going with you on your mission."

"Mission? No can do. I have a job. You know, ferrying the souls across the Styx. Father and son gig. I can't let my dad down."

"Such a good son, it makes me sick." Lucifer gagged. "You remind me of my boy, Christopher. He's such a disappointment that way too. But no worries about your father. Charon said I was more than welcome to have you. Actually, his exact words were, 'Take that clumsy idiot and make a man of him, would you?' So you see, you're good to go out into the wilds with Valaska here and count minions."

"Excuse me?" The geeky fellow blinked a few times and then dug into his pocket, pulling out black-rimmed glasses that he perched on his nose.

Much as she hated to admit it, he kind of rocked the whole academic look, not that she'd let her Amazon sisters know of course. They'd mock her for finding such a weak male specimen cute.

"You are not excused. Forgiveness is for pussies," Lucifer announced.

"I wasn't asking for forgiveness, more like a repeat of what you said because I must have misunderstood. Did you say you wanted me to count minions in the wild?"

"Indeed I did. I need a proper count of all the able bodies that I can conscript in case of a conflict. War is coming," Lucifer said, his tone low and ominous.

"A war with who?"

"Who cares?" Lucifer rubbed his hands with evident glee. "All I know is it's about time. The last one was more magic based than violent, and Muriel got most of the glory from it. Damned daughter constantly making me look bad. She does a father proud. But this time, I'm going to be ready. I am really hoping for a bloody battle that I can sink my teeth into. Blood is best when it's fresh, don't you know."

"Are you out of your fucking mind?" Adexios asked.

"According to eighty-nine out of a hundred psychiatrists, yes," Lucifer replied with evident pride.

"And what about the other eleven?" Adexios asked.

"Had them reassigned to latrine duty for incompetence of course. I have a reputation to maintain after all. Mentally balanced, my hairy ass."

"Well, you'll be glad to know that this current scheme of yours is utterly nuts."

"What are you talking about? Adventure in the wild hunting down reluctant recruits. Sounds like fun to me. Count me in." Valaska always did enjoy roughing it.

"Would you stop saying you're in," Adexios

exclaimed with a sharp look in her direction. "Do you have any idea what an impossible task he's given us? The wilds are uncharted for a reason. They keep growing, which means we'll never be able to cover them all and document all the demons hiding in them."

"He does have a point," Lucifer said, agreeing. "It's total busy work, but I had to do something. Your dad is too nice"—cue the gagging noise—"to tell you this, but he thinks you're not cut out for the ferrying souls business."

"And he's just now realizing this?" Adexios rolled his eyes. "I could have told him that the first time I capsized the boat in still water. I don't know why he came to you with his concerns. Dad could have said something to me. He wouldn't have hurt my feelings. I'm glad the truth is finally out in the open because now I don't feel obligated to follow in his footsteps—"

"Does he have feet?" Valaska couldn't help but ask.

"Fine. Follow in his robe, or whatever you want to call it. I can concentrate on another job. No need to find one for me, boss, but thank you. I appreciate you wanting to help me out."

Smoke began to wisp from Lucifer's ears. "Would you stop it with the manners? Who the hell says thank you? You know, I was almost ready to let you off the hook, but instead, I think it is time you remembered who the fuck is boss. I'm the boss, and I say you're going to the wilds to count fucking demons. And that's final."

With a poof of brimstone smoke, Lucifer vanished from sight, leaving Adexios with a dropped jaw.

"Way to go, geek boy. Now you've pissed off the big guy."

"Oh, please. Don't tell me you bought that act. Lucifer is up to something."

"Yeah, he wants us to find demons. Sounds like fun."

He glared at her. "Mucking around in the swamps and ash forest is not fun. It's dirty. Hot. And lacking in all amenities."

He said that like it was a bad thing. "Exactly. Don't worry, nerd boy. I'll make sure none of the big bad monsters hurt you."

But she didn't guarantee she'd protect him from herself. Making her negative partner scream yes instead of no was just the kind of challenge she could sink her teeth into.

I wonder how he feels about biting.

Chapter Three

"Manners are for pussies. As are dicks."
Lucifer's unofficial thirteenth commandment.

In the blink of an eye, Lucifer reappeared in his office sporting a wide smile. He had a reason to be well pleased with himself, given the meeting had gone more or less how he expected.

Adexios resented him—which totally meant he was in the running for shittiest boss of the year.

Valaska was looking for violence and trouble—and she'd totally find some, even if Lucifer had to manufacture it.

And was it him or did he detect a spark between the two?

"You look entirely too pleased with yourself."

The yelp Lucifer let out had nothing to do with the fact that his fiancée had snuck up on him. "Dammit, woman. How many times do I have to tell you to wear that lovely bracelet I got you?"

"You mean the one with bells?" Gaia held up her wrist. "I am. But I've charmed it into silence."

"Why would you do that?"

"Because it bothered my roses."

Liar. She'd silenced it so she could sneak up on him. But he appreciated her verbal sin because he knew she did it just for him. How he loved this woman. He just didn't like to mention it aloud. Feelings, much like courtesy, were for pussies.

"Well, you shouldn't just pop in like that. I could have been conducting an important meeting. How would it look if you just sashayed in, whenever you wanted, interrupting shit?"

"Like I was disrespecting you, which, in turn, means I would have required correction." Gaia shot him a sassy smile, and he almost tossed her on his desk to have his way with her.

"Incorrigible wench."

"Your wench."

"Mine." How he loved coveting and possessing things, especially someone as spectacular as Mother Earth.

In your face, brother. And God thought he was so hot just because he was dating Diana, that moon goddess chick.

"I love it when you get all growly. Come over here, lover."

"Wench, put your seductive wiles on hold. I am conducting serious business."

"Matchmaking again?" she asked dryly.

"Of course. Is it my fault I have a talent for it?" Lucifer had no modesty when it came to admitting his strengths.

"You're not supposed to force people to fall in love."

"Why not? It worked with you." He waggled his brows and leered.

"You didn't force me. Against my better judgment, and despite all the therapy sessions and spells, I just couldn't help myself. You're like crack to my heart."

His gaze narrowed. "Did you just compare me to a highly addictive, dangerous drug?"

"Yes."

"*Mon amour.*" He couldn't help but swoop in for a kiss that went from her wrist, up her bare arm, and to the hollow of her neck.

Gaia giggled. "Luc, you are so bad."

"The baddest." And horniest.

Also the most blue balled seeing as how she stepped away from him before he could manage to strip her and sink balls deep into her delicious sex.

"About Adexios, you aren't seriously sending him out to count demons in the wild? It's impossible and a waste of his talent," she said.

Lucifer rolled his eyes in a very duh expression. "I know the boy is too smart for that. However, I couldn't tell him the real reason I needed him out there."

"You're still searching for that thing that popped in from that other dimension, aren't you? I thought you told me not to worry my pretty pubic curls about it."

"And I still don't want you to worry. I will handle it. This is man's work." Chauvinism, alive and well in Hell.

"Handle what? Did you find anything out?"

He grimaced. "No, and this despite the fact that I've scoured the circles. I've had Nefertiti cast her magic. I've had all the prophecy makers brought in and questioned. Goats have been sacrificed then barbecued. Tea, drunk by the gallon so we can read the leaves. My people have been scouring the rag sheets and listening to the rumor mills. Nothing has shown up."

"Maybe because there is nothing to worry about."

He could tell she didn't believe that lie either. Something had come out of that interdimensional rift during that fiasco with the mermaids. Something evil. Something that threatened his kingdom.

And he wanted to find it so he could demolish it.

"I know what will help take your mind off things." Gaia cast him a sassy look as she bent over his desk, presenting her bottom, a creamy bottom that she exposed by having a warm, fragrant breeze lift her filmy green skirt. "I was a bad girl today, lover."

"How bad?" he asked, his mood, along with his cock, lifting.

"Let's just say I need you to punish me."

No one could ever accuse Lucifer of not giving his woman what she needed. And she was right. It did help him forget about everything. Even the fact that he'd forgotten to give his newest matchmaking pair some recent information about the wilds.

Chapter Four

"If a damned one gives you lip, toss them overboard. The monsters love a squeaky toy." A tip overheard between Ferrymen.

What am I doing here? Not for the first time, Adexios had to wonder.

Smart guys didn't go wandering around in the wilds with an Amazon woman who kept hoping aloud that they'd "run into trouble," and then threatening to "hunt trouble down," if it didn't find them.

He still couldn't quite fathom how he'd ended up in this place. Adexios only vaguely recalled the hustle and bustle to get ready with Valaska prodding him to get his "skinny ass moving." The last few days of him stalling, but being unable to shirk, seemed like a bad dream. A nightmare really that saw him entering a ring-to-ring portal transporter, followed by a long walk—because the enslavement of animals to carry lazy, entitled asses was wrong according to his companion. However who cared—other than his poor blistered feet—how he got here when the end result had led him here, to the edge of Hell.

Well, technically it was the edge of the ninth circle, but given that past this ring stretched the untamed and mostly unmapped wilds, he might as well say it was the end.

The end of me too more than likely. He'd already almost died once when he tripped going in the portal and was spat out the other side, head first, which, in itself, wasn't new. In the course of his life, he'd landed on his head too many times to count. However, the jagged head of the mace held by the portal guard would have probably hurt had he skidded an inch farther.

But that was yesterday. Today he faced a new challenge. Leaving the dubious safety of Hell for the certain danger of the wilds.

Before he took that moment-defining step over the boundary separating the zones, he paused. *I don't know if I can do this.*

"Why are you stopping?" Valaska asked, halting herself to peer at him over her shoulder.

He took a moment before replying, shoving his glasses up on his nose, wishing he'd worn more antiperspirant, given his linen shirt already stuck to his skin. "Aren't you worried about setting foot in *there*?"

Her brow wrinkled. "No."

"Aren't you concerned by the possibility we'll get lost?"

"No. I have an excellent sense of direction."

Good thing one of them had that. Adexios had an ability to get lost sometimes between the supermarket and his apartment. He was convinced gremlins were conspiring and moving street signs on him.

"What of the danger we'll face?"

"A girl needs exercise."

"And what if there's too many foes to beat?"

"Stop thinking so much. If it is our time to die, then we shall do so with glory. If it is our time to shine, then we shall emerge victorious."

Trust in fate? Why not? It hadn't killed him yet.

But then, of course, she would say the one thing to make him stumble as he finally took the deciding step.

"And should you not make it through, I will do

my best to bring your body home to your family."

Thunk.

He met the ground of the wilds face first. Good news? His glasses didn't break—at a young age, his parents had invested in the sturdiest frames they could find. He also observed that this dirt proved just as hard and unyielding as the one he liked to say hello to on a regular basis back home.

"If you're done communing with nature, could we get moving? I'd like to be well into the interior before nightfall. I hear the farther in we go, the bigger the beasts."

That announcement alone should have sent him to his feet, running in the opposite direction. However, having faced down most of the Styx sea monsters, he found that didn't scare him as much as it should have. The prospect, though, of spending days, maybe weeks, alone with Valaska terrified him.

Was it possible to desire a woman who, at the same time, made him shiver? In fear, or longing…maybe both?

Scrambling to his feet, he took a moment to dust himself off while she rolled her eyes and tapped her foot impatiently.

"Shall we?" he asked, sweeping an arm in a grand gesture toward the faint path that led yonder.

"About time," she grumbled, hefting her spear and taking long strides into the dark jungle.

Hoping nothing lurked in the treetops, he followed her.

For hours, they trekked through the green morass. Hell's version of a sun didn't penetrate the thick canopy much, leaving it a dank and damp place. Life thrived in this hellacious ash forest, the trees big monoliths that stretched high and whose gnarly trunks were thick, thick enough to hide any number of predators.

Eyes constantly darting, Adexios watched for danger. He almost turned blue he held his breath so many times. Yet, nothing popped out at them. Not even a four-eared, flame-tailed hell bunny.

Of the insects, though, they saw many. But at least they were of a normal-sized variety, easily slapped to death. But rumor had it the farther in a person lost themselves, the bigger and more aggressive the bug life got.

Around the noon hour—and yes, he knew what time it was because he'd brought a watch—he found himself a thick-looking log and, draping a plastic tarp he'd brought over it, seated himself.

Valaska, who'd continued a few paces, didn't take long to notice. She turned and, upon spotting him sitting cross-legged on the log, asked, "What are you doing?"

Pausing in the process of yanking a plastic-sealed container from his bag, he replied, "Having lunch."

"You brought food?" she said, her tone pitched with incredulity.

"Well, yeah. Didn't you?"

"Not the kind that needs a fork."

Having twirled some pasta on the said offensive utensil, he popped it in his mouth and chewed before replying. "What's wrong with eating leftover spaghetti?"

"We're on a quest. You're supposed to bring proper food for the field such as ration bars, freeze-dried meals, smoked jerky, trail mix."

"You can eat those, if you like. As for me"—he took another bite and chewed with obvious pleasure—"I'll stick to Ma's packed lunches."

"How many meals did you manage to pack in that bag? And how long do you think they'll last without refrigeration?"

"First off, they're not in my bag. They're in my mom's fridge."

Judging by the glazed look in her eyes, he'd lost her.

"This is a special knapsack. A going-away present from my parents. It's got a space-time continuum pocket that leads right to a shelf in my parents' fridge. Mom was worried about me not getting the proper kind of food and wasting away to skin and bones."

Actually, her exact words were, "we don't need you turning into your father."

"So, they made sure I wouldn't starve. You're more than welcome to have some." He reached in and pulled out another container. "Here, take this one. It's labeled goulash, homemade of course. It's my dad's favorite dish."

"No." Valaska shook her head, sending her blonde ponytail whipping. "Keep your food and your weird pocket. I am an Amazon. We feed ourselves with what we can scrounge from the land."

"Like what?" he asked, looking around and making a grimace. "I don't see anything edible around here."

Pulling forth the knife she had strapped on her hip, Valaska slashed at some foliage. "This is similar to salad." She shoved some in her mouth and chewed. "Just a bit more bitter. But it's got tons of vitamins."

He poked at a meatball in his dish and held it up. "This is one hundred percent beef protein, imported from the mortal realm, mixed with onion, spices, and then fried before being added to the sauce." He popped it in his mouth and let out a groan. "Delicious."

"Delicious is a nicely smoked piece of pitmoose." She pulled a piece of jerky out of a pouch at her waist and grabbed it with her lips. She worried at the tough strip, twisted and ground at it with her teeth until a piece broke off. Then she chewed, and chewed, and chewed. "Mmm. Nothing like it."

"Well, since you're enamored with eating al fresco, don't let me bother you. I'll just finish my pasta, and pie, in silence, envying you the leather and weeds you're dining on."

At her glare, he couldn't help but laugh, and yes, he might have purposely enjoyed his meal more than he should have, mostly because she regarded him with such hunger. Such desire…

It didn't matter that she coveted his food and not him. His body didn't make a distinction. His cock swelled, and all his nerve endings lit with awareness.

When she said, "Don't move," just as he was about to spoon another chunk of apple pie in his mouth, he froze.

She stalked toward him, gaze intent.

What did she plan? What would she do?

He held his breath, waiting to find out.

Valaska leaned down, low enough that he could see into the shadowy vee of her cleavage.

Adexios swallowed hard.

She drew close, so close he could have narrowed the gap between them and tasted her lips.

"Stay still," she admonished.

No problem. He was turned to petrified stone once he saw the knife.

Chapter Five

"Never let them see death coming, unless you want to hear them cry." Advice from Ruthless Mary after a few grogs.

Her geeky companion's eyes widened behind his lenses as her knife left its sheath. He opened his mouth. Determined to silence him, she plastered her lips over his while, at the same time, striking at the snake dangling overhead.

Thing was, while the ploy to keep him quiet worked, it had an unintended side effect. Her libido fired up.

His lips, while soft appearing, weren't so compliant when it came to kissing. Her repressed geek knew how to make the most of a kiss.

Sensual slides. A tug of a lower lip. Hot, panting breath.

Completely wrong time, wrong place, wrong guy. Valaska pulled away from him and saw his eyes blink at her owlishly from behind his glasses.

"What was that?" he asked.

"Me saving your life. And this," she said as she snuck the bite of pie hanging precariously from his spoon, "is my reward." Not exactly the reward a certain throbbing spot between her legs would have liked, but it would have to do.

Odd how the stolen bit didn't taste as good as the taste she'd gotten from his lips.

Leaning away from him, she pulled out a rag and wiped the gore from her knife. It was then Adexios noted the severed snakehead on the log beside him.

To his credit, he didn't flinch or scream. To her surprise, he leaned closer for a look.

"This is interesting," he noted, using his spoon to turn the head so he could peek at the eyes. "I don't believe this species is native to Hell."

"I'm glad you find that interesting," she snapped, only a little miffed he showed more interest in the dead reptile than the kiss they'd shared.

The least he could do is act in awe for a little while longer.

And now she was whining like the younger girls in her tribe who'd just discovered boys.

Ugh. She was a mature warrior who didn't place much stock in kisses. Apparently, neither did he.

"It is interesting because, if I'm not mistaken, this bad boy is from the mortal plane."

"From Earth?" She frowned. "But how?"

"There are a few possibilities. One, someone smuggled one back in and either lost it or set it free."

"The Hell-Eco Preservation Society won't like that." Those nutjobs were all about keeping Hell the most awful place to live. Any measures to stem the flow of ash by installing filters or introducing outside species to control the hellroaches and other pests were soundly met with opposition. Hell was hell. If you didn't like it, then don't fucking sin. "What's the other possibility?"

"An unauthorized rift between our world and the mortal plane."

"Wouldn't Lucifer know about it?"

"Not if someone created it out here in the wilds."

"But the amount of power needed to do that—"

"Would be stupendous. I know. Other than

Lucifer, Gaia, and God, there aren't many beings that could summon the kind of power to create something permanent like a portal between planes."

"Maybe it was a quickie rip and something slipped through."

"Maybe," he mused aloud, but he didn't sound convinced, and she noted he took even more note than before of their surroundings.

What did he see that had him looking so pensive?

With their meal finished—hers leaving her stomach less than happy, the jerk. How dare he make her scrounging pale in comparison—they set off again. But this time, she didn't lead the way. It seemed her geeky companion, with the discovery of the Earth snake, had found an enthusiasm for their mission that he lacked before.

With him ahead of her, she found herself not only paying attention to their surroundings but his butt.

As butts went, it wasn't big, and his khakis weren't tight. Yet, his tall, lanky frame, and the way his waist tapered to it, drew attention, especially since he strode with confidence.

How strange. Whereas before he'd regarded their surroundings with suspicion, expecting monsters to jump out from every pocket of shadow, now he strutted, pausing only long enough to peruse more closely a spider on a leaf and a rather vivid pink flower that seemed out of place. Now that he'd put on his observer persona, he had all the courage necessary.

And as to the handful of predators that crept behind him, and down trees, looking to pounce on this man who would disturb their home, she quietly disposed of them.

Not that there were many.

Certainly not enough compared to the stories

she'd heard about this place. Those of her tribe who'd wandered the wilds in search of glory had returned with grandiose stories of the non-stop battles they'd fought against the beasts that lived within.

Had her tribe mates exaggerated, or was there something wrong?

Around mid afternoon, the latter seemed more likely as the trees thinned, but not because there were fewer of them. More because they appeared to be dying.

Gray trunks, barren branches, and a ground littered in moldy leaves. This was not the appearance of a thriving forest.

Adexios stopped abruptly. Curious, she came alongside, but before she could speak, he pointed at a hump, covered in a dusting of ash, just ahead on the faint trail.

When the lump twitched, she drew her sword.

"I do believe we've found our first demon," he whispered.

A demon that wouldn't live long enough to serve his lord.

Valaska stood over the barely breathing body and feared touching it, with reason. The demon's once-red skin, which in healthy specimens shone bright, the fiery color the unmistakable mark of a fire imp, had faded to a rusty orange streaked with gray. However, it was the blotches and open sores that oozed yellow pus that kept her from touching.

Adexios showed no such fear. He knelt beside the creature and placed his hand on the dry, cracked skin of its forehead. "He's not feverish. A bad sign for his kind."

"Is he contagious?"

"No." Said with utter certainty.

"How can you be so sure?"

He flicked her a glance. He must have seen the doubt in her face and offered her a reassuring smile. "These wounds are burn marks. The skin eaten away as if from some acidic substance or hot source. Whatever he came in contact with must have contained something poisonous to his kind. See how the edges are gray, and there are no signs of healing? His immune system has been compromised. It's why his body is shutting down and his fire is burning low."

"He's dying."

"Yes."

"How do you know all this? I thought you were simply a ferry man, not a doctor."

"I am a boatman to the souls. Not a very good one though, and that is why I spend my off-duty hours studying."

"Studying?" Her nose wrinkled.

"You needn't say it like it's such a dirty word," he chided with a chuckle. "Some of us prefer to exercise our brains instead of our bodies."

"So, since you're so smart, geek boy, what did this to him?" Because whatever it was, if it proved that virulent to demons, then it would prove deadly to them with their more fragile, humanish traits.

Amazon women might prove tough, but they were mortal.

"I have no idea what did this, but maybe this fellow can tell us?"

"And how will you manage that? He's unconscious. Are you going to read his mind?"

"I have something that should wake him up." Adexios pulled a flask from a pocket in his knapsack and wiggled the stopper from it. He tipped it over and let a few drops hit the demon's lips.

For a moment, nothing happened. Then the imp

swallowed.

Its eyes shot open, dark orbs with jagged red streaks. It sucked in a deep breath and sat upright with a yell. "Fuck a duck!"

"I don't think they'd like that," Adexios replied, with the most serious mien.

She almost giggled.

Get a hold of yourself. This was not a time for mirth.

Taking a look around, the demon took stock of their surroundings before facing Adexios with a suspicious frown. "Who are you?" growled the red imp. "And what did you give me? It felt cold. But good."

"I gave you a few drops of water from the Garden of Life."

In spite of herself, Valaska was impressed. The stuff was extremely hard to acquire. Mother Nature held it under strict lock and key, the rumors declaring that too much of it released in the world would unbalance the natural order.

Things had to die in order for others to be born.

But, in spite of Mother Nature's rigid stance, some of the valuable water still ended up on the white market, and those damned angels who peddled it drove a hard bargain.

"I need more," the demon demanded.

Adexios shook his head.

Not the answer the imp wanted. It lunged for Adexios.

The stupid man didn't move. He let the imp grab a hold of him and yank him close.

"Give. Me. More."

"I have no more," Adexios lied. And she knew it was a lie for she'd seen how carefully he poured and then stoppered the bottle before tucking it behind it, hidden from sight. "Even if I did, given the severity of your wounds, you'd need more than a few flasks to clear you of this malignancy."

The demon snarled, showing sharp teeth, and yet Adexios didn't flinch.

"Getting mad at me won't change things. Tell me what happened."

"Why? I'm going to die. Who the fuck cares?" the demon whined, releasing Adexios and lying back on the ground with a dramatic fling of his upper body. "Why should I tell you?"

"You should tell me so I can stop it from happening again."

The demon said nothing, staring instead at the dying jungle canopy over him.

Valaska knew the right words to make him talk. "We will give you vengeance. We shall spill blood in your name. Make those who did this to you scream in agony."

"Really?" This drew the imp's interest, and a sickly smile stretched its cracked, black lips.

"Yes. I give you my word as a warrior that we will hunt thy enemy and smite it." She punched the palm of her hand with a fist.

"Tell us what happened," Adexios prompted.

"Happened?" The demon cackled, the sound feeble and ending with a wet, gasping cough. It seemed the initial adrenaline the water had given him had already worn off. "I will tell you what happened. Impossible beauty. Purest evil. I thought I'd found rapture."

"But?"

"Decay. Despair. Darkness." The imp's eyes widened, and the black orbs took on a milky cast. "We must flee. Hide. Now. We must run." The demon bolted upright and wobbled on his taloned feet.

Adexios grabbed him lest he fall over. "Why must we run and hide?"

Black ichor began to leak from the demon's eyes and nose. His breathing emerged in choppy gasps. "Death is coming. Death is here. And it looks like…looks…like…"

The demon sagged and fell backward, the sudden slump too abrupt for Adexios, who lost his grip.

Dropping to his knees, Adexios leaned close, very close as the demon uttered his last dying breath and words.

Valaska didn't hear it, but judging by Adexios' grim expression he had.

Getting to his feet, he walked away from the corpse. He gathered his things.

"What are you doing?"

"We have to go."

"Wait. What did he say? What did this to him?"

Adexios faced her, his face still grim, but not afraid. Was that determination she spied in his eyes?

"The demon said *she* is coming. And she intends to remake our world."

Chapter Six

"Don't talk to the passengers. You'll ruin the mystique." From the official Ferryman's guide.

The demon's death and warnings put a damper on any conversation. Oh wait, that was already happening before.

For some reason, Adexios found himself tongue-tied around Valaska. Anyone else, he had a snappy retort—just ask his dad.

"Son, why are the damned arriving wet?"

"I might have accidentally hit that whirlpool on account of I hate this job!"

On second thought, maybe not snappy, but at least he had a reply.

With his friends, he always found a topic of interest, one of the more popular ones being the decaying social structure of the rings—a debate going on now for a few centuries according to Ol' Pete, who'd started it back during the Spanish Inquisition.

When conversing with his mom, it was usually something along the lines of, "When are you settling down?" Apparently when the right woman came along and crazy glued his feet to the floor was not the right answer. That cost him dessert for a week.

Still though, he knew how to hold up his end of a conversation, and it drove him nuts that he kept hesitating saying something to Valaska. It wasn't as if he didn't have questions: *What's it like being an Amazon? How young did you start your training? Is it true Amazon warriors kill their men after they've taken their seed? And does the blonde on your head match the carpet below?*

Wait a second. That wasn't his thought.

For a moment, he looked around, suspicion in his gaze, but the person who would have uttered such a thing was nowhere to be seen. But Adexios never put anything past the Lord of Mischief. The devil had a picture under the definition of devious. He also had one under troublemaker and meddler, which was what Adexios suspected was at play.

If Lucifer harbored any mistaken ideas about getting Adexios to pair off with a woman so he could make super minions, then he could just forget it. He wasn't about to become the newest victim of the devil's matchmaking game—even if Valaska was ridiculously hot. Hot didn't make her healthy for him. The woman had thighs strong enough to crush a man if he dared get between her legs.

Sigh.

What a way to die.

Speaking of dying, he really should pay attention to their surroundings, given he'd almost stepped into a very strange puddle.

He held up his arm to halt Valaska. "Stop. Don't touch this."

"Yes, let us fear the innocuous pool of clear water. It is so obviously dangerous," Valaska said in an utterly dry tone.

"And how do you know it isn't?" he retorted. "Look around you. Have you seen how many of these puddles have started cropping up?" Some almost pond-sized at more than eight feet across, but none of them very deep. "Doesn't it seem odd to you?"

She rolled her shoulders. "It's a puddle of water.

They happen when it rains. Give it a few hours. It will probably evaporate."

"If this were a normal puddle, I'd agree. But this body of water wasn't created by a rain shower. At least not one that happened recently. Look around, if it had been left by a natural weather phenomenon, there'd be signs of moisture, and yet look." He crouched and grabbed at the loose and dry soil, rubbing it between his fingers. It left dusty marks, and a weak puff of breeze blew some of the smaller particles loose. "This ground hasn't seen moisture in days, if not weeks."

"I knew that," she grumbled.

Did he spot a hint of red in her cheeks?

Kneeling at the edge of the clear water basin in his path, he stared and frowned. "This is very strange."

"What's the matter?"

The shallow depression in the dirt held the water much like a bowl would, but nothing else. "Don't you find it odd that you can see the bottom?" he asked.

Leaning over him, she peeked. "It's not deep. Of course, we can see the bottom."

"But we shouldn't and for several reasons. One, according to surveys of this area—"

"Hold, I thought the wilds were unmapped. You bitched about that a few times when we were prepping to come."

Bitching? No, merely pointing out the impossibility of their mission.

"Most of the wilds are uncharted, but this section we're in, being so close to the border and to the last portal town in the ninth ring, is actually decently documented. I studied those maps before our departure."

"Nerd."

"I prefer the term informed."

"Getting feisty with me, geek boy?"

Not intentionally, but now that she mentioned it, yes, he would like to get feisty, with her, wearing no clothes. But that wasn't what he replied. "I am simply reporting facts. And the fact is, according to maps, we should have reached the edge of the rainforest and entered the swamplands."

"So the landscape changed. Big deal. This is the wilds. It changes all the time."

"Yes and no. While the foliage might get bigger, and swamps shrink or grow depending on the season, certain things remain the same, such as the fact that clear water puddles shouldn't exist out here when the ground is much too dry. The soil should be sucking it in like a sponge. And why is there no algae growth? Or debris in any of the puddles? Add into that the fact that there is too much dead and dying foliage and a distinct lack of life."

"Lack? I saw plenty of life on our way in. Killed a few that wanted to take yours."

"Now who's acting feisty?" He wondered which of them was more surprised, him or her, at his statement.

She laughed. "Any time you wanna give me a try, geek boy, you let me know, and I'll show you just how feisty I can get."

"Could you please call me something other than geek boy? It's emasculating."

"Geek man?"

He scowled.

Her reply? Laughter. "Fine. How about Dex? Is that manly enough for you?"

"Dex is fine. Now back to these odd puddles. Notice how there are no tracks leading to them? Animals require fluids to flourish, yet I see no sign they're using this crystal-clear water to quench their thirst."

"So you think it is poisoned?"

"I don't know. It doesn't smell like poison."

"Because you've smelled so many in your life?"

"Actually yes, I have. Part of my boatman training. Believe it or not, people have tried to assassinate my dad over the years in the hopes of taking over his job."

"They obviously weren't very good at it," she said with noticeable disdain. "When someone in my tribe sets out to kill someone, they always succeed."

"Oh, some of them were good, but my dad kicks ass." Said with obvious pride. While he and his father might sometimes find themselves at odds, he still bore a strong affection and respect for the man.

"I didn't take Charon for a fighter."

Adexios didn't take offense. Not many knew about his dad's super skills. "No one does, which is why it's so awesome. But fighting isn't all he's learned to do. Over the centuries, my dad also had to watch the food we brought into the house for poison."

"And he taught you this detecting skill?"

He nodded. "Taught and helped me build a resistance to several kinds. He said, as his son, I was a target, too."

"Aren't you just the most intriguing geek ever? Very well, since you're the expert, sniff it and tell me what you smell."

Bending down, while careful to keep his hands from the edge lest it turn out to be some sort of acidic compound, he inhaled a deep breath through his nose. "I sense no bitterness. Nor nutty smells." He drew in another nose full, and his brow creased. "It kind of reminds me a bit of the Darkling Sea smell. Briny, and yet, without the algae undertone."

"For fuck's sake, this is taking too long. Why not

just taste it?"

"Are you insane…"

His voice trailed off as Valaska crouched. She didn't hesitate to cup a handful of the water and bring it to her lips.

She sipped from her hands and grimaced. "Ugh."

"Are you all right? Is your mouth burning? Are you in pain?"

"No pain other than to my palate. The stuff tastes like seawater."

"Seawater?" Given she wasn't convulsing, sweating, or hitting the ground with eyes rolled back, he judged it safe enough to sample a sip.

His turn to grimace. "Oh yeah. That's salty all right, but that makes no sense. How would seawater make it out here? How did it form into so many little puddles, and why aren't they seeping into the ground?" Even more worrisome, how far did it extend?

It seemed she shared his concern. "If this is happening here, only a dozen or more miles from the edge, then what about farther in?"

"I suspect if this area isn't an anomaly, then the puddles will get larger in size. The dead trees and other bare patches will get bigger."

"If you're right, then what about the animals and other stuff that relies on the swamp lands and plants?"

"They'll die, or they're already dead." Or so he assumed, even if he'd yet to see any remains other than the one demon they'd come across.

"Do you think this is what killed that fire imp?" Valaska asked. Judging by the worried line on her forehead, she was really hoping the water wasn't the cause of that demon's death.

With a shake of his head, he allayed her fear. "No, whatever got that imp resembled a burn. If this were the cause, you'd be feeling it."

"I'd like to make sure." She stuck out her tongue. "Does it look all right to you?"

More than all right. But if she wanted to test it and make sure it was working properly, he had something she could lick.

Thank hell he still crouched lest she see the effect she had on him. "Looks fine," he muttered.

"So any ideas on what we should do now?"

"Do? How about worry about what this all means?" he said, taking out an empty jar from yet another one of his pockets and scooping some of the liquid in it.

"If the smart guy is worried, then I guess I should be too. That is unless you think I can beat these puddles with a sword?"

"Uh, no," he said rather starkly.

"Knock-out punch?" she asked hopefully.

"Still a no." Replied while wondering if she was joking about actually physically fighting puddles.

"So let me ask you how I'm supposed to fight water and burning shit that can kill even an ornery fire demon."

"You can't fight them. In order to beat this blight on the wilds, we need to find the source."

"And then I can kill something?" she asked with an eager lilt.

"If there is something to kill. Keep in mind that any being strong enough to change the landscape of the wilds is someone to be feared. It could be that the skills of a warrior aren't what we'll need. We might need magic to beat magic."

"Ugh, a sorcerer fight. Those suck unless they've raised the dead. They make worthy opponents so long as they don't ooze on you."

He shot her a startled glance and was blown away at the grin she bestowed upon him. Full of good humor, it transformed her from an intimidating blonde warrior goddess to an intimidating, fucking smoking-hot blonde warrior goddess.

Face it, smiling or not, Valaska was what he wanted, wanted even more than a caffeine-laced coffee.

"Why are you looking at me funny? I'm serious, you know. Decomposing corpse is hell to get out of leather. It reeks for weeks."

He shook his head and chuckled. "I don't think I've ever heard someone speak so honestly before. It's refreshing."

"Shh!" She held her finger to her lips and peeked around. "Don't use the H word aloud. You know who could be listening. It's not honesty; it's bitching. Complaining. Totally approved behavior by the big guy."

"Are you really that paranoid about sin?"

"Well, yeah." She rolled her eyes. "Lucifer's a stickler for perfect behavior when it comes to handing out bonuses."

"You work for him often?"

"A few jobs. He calls on my tribe quite often to help out with certain jobs that need a little extra."

"Because you have such a reputation for being fierce and unrelenting."

She laughed. "That and the fact we apparently make great television. HBC has a reality show that follows our exploits. *Irons Tits, the Amazon Smackdown.* Ever seen it?"

Yes. But he wouldn't admit it. It was one of his guilty pleasures, although he didn't recall seeing Valaska on it. Then again, the face paint the warriors wore—thick eyeliner, dark eye shadow and bright lipstick—could really transform a woman.

"Sorry, I don't think I've had the pleasure."

"Apologizing again?" She tsked him. "Look at you, really trying to get on Satan's last nerve. Brave guy."

"Not really. I ignore the smaller sins in favor of getting points for the big ones." Such as the time he'd accidentally forgotten a soul on the departure shore. It happened. To him at any rate. And it wouldn't have been so bad if the damned soul hadn't wandered off and haunted a subway system for a few months.

Boy, did he get in trouble for that situation. Apparently, he'd broken some major ferryman rule. But on the upside, that subway's rat problem disappeared by the time the bounty hunters dragged the damned soul back.

"Raking in Lucifer's favor with big sins. Interesting strategy. But we are way off topic. You believe there is someone creating these puddles."

"No, I said there might be. These could also be the result of some strange, yet entirely natural, phenomenon caused by a lack of pollution in Hell or a crack in the hozone."

"Things we can't fight." She spun from him and walked away a few paces, stopping before one of the larger liquid-filled basins.

She didn't say anything or move for a few minutes.

It didn't take a genius to see the gears in her head churning. Why did she seem so torn?

"Is something wrong, Valaska?"

She sighed. "Yeah. Given the initial mission we've been sent on has drastically changed due to our discoveries, it is my belief we should turn back."

The answer startled him. "Turn back? Did you sniff some swamp gasses without sharing?" Their hallucinogenic properties were well known—if noxious smelling at first. "Why would we leave when we've only just begun our exploration? Not even a day in and we've discovered incredible things. We can't stop. We need to keep going. To find out the truth of how these puddles are coming into creation." And wow that was said with much more gusto than necessary. Maybe *he'd* sniffed some swamp gasses.

"I agree, yet, at the same time, don't. Yes, we found cool shit, but it's shit we should report."

Valaska turning down adventure because she had an incredible desire to file paperwork? He narrowed his gaze at her. "Hold on a second. Before, when our quest involved a high level of danger looking for minions in the wild, everything was fine. But now, even though we've yet to encounter anything more vicious than an out-of-place boa snake, a dying imp, and salt water, you want to quit?"

She bit her lip, and he could tell she had to force her head to nod.

"What a load of bullshit."

"Dex, such language."

"Don't go changing the subject. I know what's going on here, and I don't fucking believe it. You've been told to not let me get hurt."

At least she didn't lie. Nor did she duck her head in shame. Boldly meeting his gaze, she smiled. "Actually, letting you get hurt was considered okay. It builds character."

"Did Lucifer say that to you?" Or his dad? His dad always did say he'd have to get tougher. Of course, Dad also had an insane obsession with making sure Adexios got enough calcium. *For strong bones.*

"It wasn't Lucifer who said that thing about character. It's an Amazon teaching. We are trained to believe pain only makes you stronger. So a little pain on our quest was good. But I had to promise to not let you get killed."

"I didn't think Lucifer cared."

"He doesn't."

Of course not. "My dad," Adexios stated with assurance.

Blonde hair went whipping from side to side. "Try again. You're close."

"You listened to my mom?" His exclamation emerged a tad high-pitched. "Why the hell would you do that?"

"She cornered me with the most perfectly grilled bird leg, lightly seasoned and so juicy."

"You turned on me for rotisserie poultry?"

"And a tankard of warm apple cider."

Oh, the cider. "The smuggled kind from the mortal plane I'll wager. I see you brought out the big guns, Mother," he mused aloud.

"So you see? See how she attacked me? But I'll have you know I was resisting 'til that point," Valaska admitted with vehemence. But then her smile drooped. "Until she brought out the homemade chocolate and mint chip ice cream."

"Oh, Mother. Not the ice cream."

A frozen confection in Hell wasn't an easy-to-find commodity, especially for a warm world that had issues keeping power on. Not to mention that mortal appliances, with their reliance on science, didn't work very reliably in the pit. Something about the esoteric waves and the clogging abilities of the ash making them explode. And, in a few rare cases, absorbing their owner and coming to life.

Lucifer still had yet to recover the car that went on a killing spree and inspired a famous novel.

Personally, Adexios didn't think Lucifer tried too

hard to locate that missing murderous soul, not given the scale model he had built, which sat in a place of pride on the bookshelf in his office.

"So you agreed to utterly humiliate me for ice cream."

"With caramel sauce."

"Is that all?" he mocked.

"And a cherry."

He glared at her.

"Okay, there were two cherries, plus whipped cream. But now can't you see why I agreed?"

Yes. But he didn't forgive her or his mother. Chin tilted, in his most frosty voice, he said, "I'm a grown man. I don't need you or my mother making decisions for me."

"I agree."

He blinked at her. "Agree? About what?"

"That you should totally defy your mother and cut those apron strings. As well as let your hair grow out."

He reached up to touch his short locks. "You think so?"

"Yes, but do it another day. Even if it weren't for your mother, I'd suggest we go back. This puddle situation is important news. The Dark Lord will want to know. We should return to the last village and report it. Together."

He almost agreed and then gave a head shake. No. Something of import was happening here. Something big. Possibly deadly. Adexios might not have wanted to come here in the first place, he might fear the danger they'd encounter, but he wasn't a coward.

If something threatened the safety of Hell, his family, his friends, then he owed it to them to discover exactly what.

"You can pussy out if you want, but I'm going on. Something's happening out here. And I don't think we have time to ignore it and wait for the Department of Unnatural Disasters to fill out the paperwork necessary to get a team out here. Time is of the essence. I'm going ahead."

Valaska cocked her head and eyed him with curiosity. "You'd go alone into danger?"

"Yes. Someone needs to put a stop to what's happening."

Damn, that almost sounded fucking heroic. Later he'd have to remind Valaska to not mention anything about that speech to Satan. The devil would have a conniption for sure.

"I like a man with big balls." And to his chagrin, she dropped her gaze to his crotch.

He shifted his knapsack in front of it because he just couldn't seem to armor himself against the Amazon goddess and her unintentional allure.

She is just a woman.

A woman with a brilliant gaze, silken wheat-blonde hair, and a body that could crush a man.

He gave his head a shake. He needed to stop letting his awe, which was a polite word for lust, control him. Or, as Lucifer would have said, *Time to stop the brain farts because all the blood in my head keeps going to my dick.*

It was rather embarrassing, and also painful, just how easily she managed to arouse him. It wasn't as if Adexios was an innocent virgin. His dad had made sure of that when he hooked him up with a pair of damned twins who brokered a deal to reduce their penance.

After that eye-opening experience, he'd gone on to bed his fair share of women, okay three, but still he knew his way around a woman's body. He could have experienced more if he'd wanted to. Many ladies—and that was being generous—were determined to get in his pants to see what he hid. Once he realized this, he put a stop to it, especially since, while the ones he did sleep with were happy with his size and skill, they also left his bed disappointed because he was so, as one girl put it, 'Normal looking'.

Given he was far from a virgin—a carnal sin that earned him brownies—he should have been able to deal with this blonde beauty without any problem. And yet, he couldn't help but sport wood every time she got near.

I need to take control of this situation—and her.

"You know what? You're not going back to the last town. Neither of us is. We are going to move ahead and gather more information." He stated this in a commanding tone he'd never heard come from his mouth.

She looked as surprised as he felt, but she didn't let shock prevent her from saying, "Forget what I said before. I'm in."

Was it wrong that he wanted to be the one to say, *I'm in*, in her that was, his balls slapping against her as he—

Hello, lust, nice to see you again. Now there was a sin he didn't seem to have a problem with.

"Shall we go and save Hell?" she queried.

"I'm in." Hunh, what did you know? It was kind of fun to say it.

Spear in hand, Valaska took the lead, which meant he got a fantastic view of her ass.

Look away. Resist her allure.

Fuck that. Enjoy the ass.

Imagine that ass naked. Bent over and…

The puddle he stepped in, that soaked him to the knees, snapped him back to his senses. Keeping his gaze averted, he took the opportunity to focus on the scenery around him.

While the oversized puddles of water didn't have any growth within them, all around other vegetation grew. It just didn't look very healthy.

While the sifting ash contributed to some of the pallor in the leaves and on the trunks, it didn't take a Hotanist—someone who specialized in Hell botany—to realize the trees and plants were dying. He'd wager the high salt content in the area was to blame.

But where was the damned salt coming from? It wasn't as if it rained from the sky or spontaneously appeared?

Did it?

Never put anything past the pit. Strange things happened all the time. It played havoc with real estate prices. One day a person could be living in hellurbia, with a jagged, wrought-iron fence and a front garden lined with thorny roses. The next, a fissure could open and the noxious gases farted by the dragon at the heart of their world could waft, causing extreme eye watering and skin color changes, not to mention tainting everything with an unmistakable stink.

Would it turn out the salty puddles were in actuality tears from some giant celestial being?

He peered at the sky, the gray haze of ash blocking the view and rendering Hell's version of a sun as nothing more than a fiery, red disk.

Dusk fell, bringing with it shadows, sore feet, and a rumble in his tummy. "I think it's time we stopped for the night."

Valaska didn't argue and even accepted his offer of some of his mom's famous fettuccine Alfredo with grilled chicken and cheese-covered bread. No garlic. Although not a vampire, his mother couldn't abide it.

As they ate in silence, Adexios contemplated

what they'd found. And what they hadn't.

Over the course of the afternoon, they'd seen the foliage retreat more and more while the salt-water dilemma grew. Where they'd currently halted, the water extended all around them in puddles no smaller than six feet across. They could still travel between them, but Adexios wondered how far they would be able to travel the next day if they continued to crowd closer.

The only good news was none of the puddles appeared very deep, no more than thigh high that they'd seen, but again, that could change the farther they went.

Of other worry was the fact that they'd also not seen a single other demon. Actually, in the last hour or more, they'd not seen any life at all. Not even any bugs.

As signs went, that wasn't a good one.

Valaska was right. They needed to report this.

Stowing away his plastic containers—back into the temporal rip for his mom to wash—he then dug in his pants pocket for his cell. "You know what, now that we've gotten a full day in, I'm going to give the boss a shout and let him know what we've found."

"You have a hellphone?"

"Well, yeah." He couldn't resist a certain duh emphasis. "Who doesn't travel with one?"

Judging by her pinched lips, she didn't. "We tend to eschew technology when out in the field."

"What do you do if you have an emergency or need to contact someone?"

"We rely on the old tried and true methods. Smoke signals work anywhere."

"If someone sees them." He shook his head. "No thanks. I think I'll stick to calling people."

"Why didn't you mention you had a phone earlier when I talked about going back?"

He shrugged. "I figured you had one, too, but

didn't want to use it."

"I don't."

"Apparently. Good thing we're not both Luddites."

"Did you just call me a name?"

Would she hit a guy with glasses? He shoved them against his face to draw attention to them just in case. "Yup."

She beamed. "About time. Although, next time you want to insult someone, could you use a word that doesn't require a dictionary?"

"How's technophobe?"

"Better. So what are you going to tell the big guy?" she asked.

"The truth."

A wide grin popped a dimple in her cheek. "You know he hates that."

"Which is what makes it so fun."

Adexios dialed before putting the phone to his ear.

Ring. Ring. The phone was answered with a grunt.

"Hello?" Adexios queried. "Lucifer?"

"Oh yeah, that's it, there's the spot." Lucifer moaned.

Had his boss butt answered?

Adexios held the phone away from his ear as the moans continued. Should he hang up?

And look like a weakling?

Never. "Hey, boss. Am I calling at a bad time?"

"Nope. Oh, oh don't stop."

"Maybe I should call back later. You sound occupied."

The moaning stopped as Lucifer laughed. "Such a prude. What's wrong, boy? You think I'm getting head?"

"Of course not. I would never think such a thing." Because thinking of his boss getting some was like thinking about the fact that his parents had done it once—and once only—to conceive him. Gross.

"Are you saying I'm too old to get head?" Lucifer growled.

"Never."

"I like head."

"I'm sure you do. You know what? I think I'm needed elsewhere." He glanced at Valaska for help, but she just smirked.

"I can still talk to you even if I'm getting a BJ you know. I'm a great multitasker."

"I'm sure you are."

"But alas, I'm not getting head."

"Of course you aren't," Adexios hastily agreed.

"Are you implying Gaia doesn't take care of me like a proper girlfriend should?"

Why was this conversation constantly derailing? He'd just called to report. "I would never think that."

"She does, you know. Why, she took care of me just last night, right before I took care of her. That cyclone off the coast of South America, my fault. When the master of lies applies his tongue, she gushes." Lucifer chuckled, and Adexios closed his eyes and wished he'd never called. "So what did you want, anyhow? Have you already finished counting my minions?"

"Of course not. We haven't even started."

"Slacker! No wonder I like you so much."

"You know what, I think I misdialed."

"Are you trying to hang up on me, boy?" Lucifer's voice turned low and ominous.

"No."

"Liar. Your parents must be so proud. So have you had any luck tracking down any wily demon bastards?"

"That's part of the reason I'm calling. We haven't found any yet. Well, actually we did find one, but he's dead now."

"What do you mean dead? I didn't send you out there to kill my recruits. Did I? I know I sent someone to kill something. I think."

Adexios rubbed his forehead. Sometimes talking with Lucifer took patience to a whole new level. "We didn't kill the fire imp. He died of something weird that got him in the wilds."

"Duh. What did you expect? You're in untamed territory."

"I know, but when I say weird, I am talking deadly-to-demons shit. There is something seriously wrong with the wilds."

"Found those salt water puddles have you?"

For a moment Adexios just stood blinking as he processed Lucifer's words. "You knew about them?"

"Of course I did. My hunters reported them a few weeks back when they started appearing."

"And you never thought to inform us before we went on this stupid mission?"

"Did I forget? My bad. I'll have to reward myself later. How are those puddles doing anyhow?"

"I don't know what your hunters told you, but they are bad news. Real bad news. They're killing things out here."

"You mean they're violent?"

"No! As in the high salt content is destroying the ecosystem. Not to mention that, since we've encountered them, we've yet to see anything alive."

"Well, that's not good. We can't have that. My hunters need their prey. I need trophies. And swamp beast rugs. Change in mission, Adexios. I hereby order you and that Amazon broad to discover the cause behind the salt-water incursion in the wild. And by the way, if during your search you happen to come across say some kind of demi god or evil force from another dimension, let me know, would you?"

Before Adexios could ask for elaboration, Lucifer hung up.

"That wily bastard," he said in a low voice.

"What's wrong, Dex?"

Wrong. Lots of things, which he should have suspected from the moment Lucifer sent them on this inane mission. "Lucifer didn't send us out here to find demons to recruit. He sent us to find whatever was unleashed when that interdimensional rip opened above the Darkling Sea a while back."

"You mean he hid our true task behind a fake one that is even more dangerous?"

"Yes!" he said, unable to hide his irritation.

"Awesome."

He glared at her beaming face, but it wasn't a glare that held much vehemence, although he did feel a lot of heat. Most of it carnal because, damn, was she gorgeous when she grinned. It made a man want to kiss those lips.

As if she'd let him. A woman like her probably dated big, burly men, not skinny nerds.

"Your enthusiasm is troubling. We are embarking on a quest for the unknown. It could cost us our lives."

Valaska twirled her sword as she answered with gusto, "Gain us glory."

"Torture us in painful, unimaginable ways."

A jab of her blade. "Test our skills."

"Is there anything I can say that will deter you?"

"Nope." She popped the p as she said it.

"Then I guess we're going exploring." Which he'd been keen on earlier in the day, but now, knowing he was part of a truly devious and satanic plot? Yeah, he'd rather watch the reality show version from his comfy chair with a bowl of popcorn.

"We won't get any more exploring done tonight," she said as she eyed the shadows creeping in around them. "Unless you've got a flamethrower in that knapsack of yours, it's time we made camp and got some shuteye."

Actually, he had the makings of a flamethrower, but he didn't let her know. Stumbling around in the dark was never a good idea.

With the decision to stop for the night made, Valaska tossed her pack on the ground, unsheathed her sword, and placed it alongside. She then lay down on the lumpy dirt, head pillowed on her bag, one hand on the hilt of her weapon and other hand holding her knife, which she slashed at a bug, the size of a fat cat, that hummed too close.

Would you look at that? Not everything had died yet. Perhaps there was still hope. For the wilds at least. He did have to wonder about Valaska though. She truly was nuts.

"This is the life," she said with a happy sigh as she stabbed the wing of yet another bloodsucker that buzzed in close. "Toss down your pack and join me, Dex."

"Uh, no thank you."

Placing his backpack on the ground, Adexios rummaged within, very aware of the fact that Valaska stared at him. His hands closed around the square object he'd paid dearly for—Nefertiti, the dark lord's most powerful sorceress, drove a hard bargain. Doing her taxes for the next decade would suck considering her waist-high pile of receipts for questionable esoteric and erotic goods. But the hours of work were worth it considering what he'd gotten in return.

From his knapsack, he retrieved a small wooden cube. Seamless but carved with symbols on five of its six faces. On the sixth side, a red X. He pressed it with his thumb and stepped back.

Magic was a wondrous thing. It took the laws of science and said, fuck them. Literally. Items that should weigh a few tons, or take a ridiculous amount of room, could, with the right spell, find themselves compressed into a tiny block that fit in the palm of his hand and weighed no more than an apple.

A tiny block that grew when activated.

"Is that a freaking cabin?" Valaska jumped to her feet and ogled as his must-have camping item expanded to its full size.

"Yes, it's a cabin, with plumbing I might add," which was why Adexios was doing taxes for a decade instead of a few years. However, the prospect of not getting his dick nipped by some kind of parasitic bug was well worth the extra price.

A pity Valaska didn't seem impressed with his expensive camping item. "This is a quest. We're expected to rough it."

A cool breeze, hinting of ocean waves, dark cold depths, and seaweed touches ruffled their hair and clothes.

As that damned soul Willy would say, especially after a few grogs, *Something wicked this way comes.*

"Yeah, if you want to sleep on the hard ground, with one eye open all night, getting eaten"—*I'll eat you*—"pricked"—*I'd prick her*—"and possibly carried off by the insect population, then be my guest. I, for one, am sleeping in a bed, surrounded by four solid, swamp-monster-proof walls. You can join me if you'd like." And by join, he didn't mean in bed.

Okay, so he lied. *You're welcome, boss.* A part of him did kind of hope she'd wind up in his bed, wearing nothing but him. Adexios would keep her warm. And flushed. And sweaty…

Mental slap. *Get your mind out of the gutter.*

Time to get inside before his blood-filled boner attracted the wrong sort of sucking.

"Come on. Let's check the place out."

Entering via the solid wood front door, that on the inside sported a heavy wooden bar for keeping things out, Adexios was struck by the simple elegance of the cabin. In many ways, it was nicer than his apartment by the wharf. Made of imported cedar wood logs on the outside, the inside continued the wooden theme with the wide plank floors.

A stone fireplace adorned one wall, a small kitchen area consisting of a stone counter and a sink spanned another. In the far corner was a closed area, the washroom facilities. Other than that, there was a couch, a big comfy chair, a small table with a pair of stools, and a great big bed.

"Dibs on the washroom." And to those who would chastise him for not offering it to the lady first? Please note he was a firm supporter of woman's lib, and that meant treating her like he would a man. He would never tell another man to use it first. Women could thank him later for his progressive and modern acceptance of women's rights. First, he had to pee.

Dropping his bag on the table, Adexios made a beeline for the bathroom. When he emerged freshly washed and dressed in the terry robe he'd found hanging on the door, he discovered Valaska hadn't followed him into the cabin.

"Don't tell me that crazy Amazon stayed outside." He stalked over to the bulletproof, Plexiglas window and peered outside. Sure enough, there was his companion, swinging her sword at a massive, multi-legged flying critter sporting a stinger on its ass that would definitely leave a mark.

He might have left her to it seeing as how she was laughing as she swung. However, given his ears could discern a hum that rose in pitch, her mutant wasp adversary was about to be joined by a squadron of friends.

Even she couldn't fight those kinds of odds.

Jabbing his hand into this bag, he removed a small aerosol can before stepping outside. Making sure to remain clear of her whistling sword swings, and the gush of bug juice as she sliced off limbs, he raised his tiny can and spritzed.

Bzzz. Brzr. *Thump*.

The oversized insect hit the ground, twitched once, twice, and then was still.

"Ah. What did you do that for? I was just getting warmed up," she whined.

"We're about to have company. So unless you're into extreme acupuncture, I might suggest we adjourn to the safety of the cabin."

"Or we could stay and battle, me wielding my mighty blade and you, your, um, fearsome spray bottle."

"Don't mock the strength and killing ability of Lucifer's cologne."

"Whatever it is, it's effective. Stay and use it against the forces of swarmhood."

"I've got hot water inside, and cocoa."

Valaska gnawed her lip, so he added, "Did I forget to mention I also have fluffy marshmallows?"

"You play dirty, Dex," she said with a sigh.

"Fine. We'll go inside." She followed him to safety—dragging her feet the entire way and casting a longing look in the direction of the almost deafening hum of wings approaching.

They'd no sooner closed the door than there was a thump. Then another.

"And this is why I hate camping," he grumbled. "Damned bugs. Hold on, if I remember the cabin's manual correctly—"

"You read the manual?"

"Of course I did. How else was I to learn of all the features it came with?"

"Experimentation. It's how I like to gain my *experience*."

A shudder went through him as she practically purred the word.

"Anyone ever tell you that you're a flirt?"

"Who's flirting? I'm just saying it like it is. Anytime you need proof, Dex, you let me know."

How about now?

Thump. Thump.

The insect invasion prevented him from saying what his dick was thinking. Instead, he located the switch with the tiny lightning bolt over it by the front door. A simple flick and he felt his skin tingle as the energy force field came to life around the house.

Zap. Zap. Zap.

The nuclear wasps, with their hive mentality, didn't immediately grasp that they were getting killed simply for touching the electrified house. But once they did, silence reigned.

With the infestation taken care of, Adexios started to relax, only to come to the realization that he was alone, in a cabin, wearing only a robe, with a bed and an Amazon hottie who was stripping off her clothes!

Chapter Seven

*"Never go into battle with dirty underpants."
Amazon rule recited to all the newbies by Skidmark
Sally.*

"What are you doing?" Dex sputtered.

In the process of stripping, she thought it quite obvious but replied anyhow. "Getting out of these dirty things so I can shower. You did say there was hot water."

"Yes, over there." He pointed in the direction of a closed-off section of the cabin while doing his best to avoid looking at her.

"Does my nakedness bother you?"

"No."

Lie. And she didn't need to see his sad attempt to hide his erection to figure out that Adexios was attracted to her, and yet for some reason, he thought he had to fight it.

He wants to fight? How sexy of him.

Challenge accepted.

Very comfortable in her skin, Valaska walked toward him with her hands full of the clothing she'd shed. Given he'd turned his back, he didn't notice her approach until she'd sidled fairly close.

He let out the cutest squeak and, being a curious kind of guy, couldn't help peeking in her direction. Once he glanced, he was a goner.

She didn't take offense that his eyes didn't

remain locked with hers. What red-blooded male wouldn't let his gaze roam and take in the splendor of her full breasts, her indented waist, and flaring hips? He didn't stare at her mound for long, even though it was clean-shaven, *for my pleasure*. Back up roved his hungry stare, stopping at her chest.

Delighted to be the focus of his attention, her nipples perked. Since he seemed so interested, she thrust her shoulders back and offered them. "Take a lick. My breasts are very sensitive to touch. I especially enjoy having them fondled and sucked."

Oops. Too forward. His cheeks heated, and he tore his gaze away. He also didn't take her up on her invitation. That had never happened before.

Was there something wrong with him? "Do you have a girlfriend?" she asked.

"No."

"A boyfriend?"

"No."

Then why was he so determined to ignore her invitation to get frisky? Unless… "Are you a virgin?" she asked.

He choked, coughing and gasping for breath. She reached over, meaning to help him, but he darted out of reach, but not before she'd grabbed the cloth of his robe, a robe she got to keep.

It seemed Dex had not tied the sash tightly, as it slid off his shoulders and hung from her hands while he gaped stupidly.

Gathering his wits, and striving for cover, in the form of his hands covering his hard-to-hide erection, he lifted his chin and said, "Would you mind returning my robe?"

Actually she did mind. She balled it up and tossed it into the fireplace. It lit with a whoosh. Bye-bye, robe.

"What did you do that for?" he exclaimed. "I was wearing that."

"Not anymore. Besides, I think you look better like this." Wearing nothing at all but his embarrassment and glasses.

"But like this is cold."

"Not for long. The fireplace is heating up. You know, if you find you're cold a lot, then maybe you should think of adding some meat to your frame. You are all skin and bones." And muscle. Every inch of him was surprisingly toned, especially his thighs.

"Mom always did say I took after my dad."

The rumors said Charon, after his many centuries of service, had dwindled into nothing but a skeleton. But no one knew for sure.

Since Dex didn't seem inclined to dive for a new set of clothes, or dive on her for that matter, she turned her back on him and tossed her things into the sink and added some water along with dish soap.

"You're washing your stuff by hand?" he asked.

Since it was obvious, she didn't reply.

"You do know there's a washer-dryer combo in the bathroom, right?"

She paused in the process of swishing her laundry. She whirled around. "That, Dex, is sad. So sad."

"Why sad?" he asked from his spot on the couch. Legs crossed, attempting to look casual, yet failing. "I like clean clothes."

"So do I."

"I also value efficiency, so while yours are still dripping in front of the fireplace in the morning, mine will be nice and toasty dry."

She couldn't help it. Her wet laundry went flying. He easily ducked the bulky corset, and her shorts, but her wadded thong? That one hit him in the face and got tangled on the frame of his glasses.

Given she mostly hung out with male warriors, usually in bars since the Amazon village had rules about letting them live there, she expected him, at the very least, to fling them back. A part of her hoped he'd snap and stride toward her, grab her in his arms, and retaliate with hot, fierce sex.

Instead, her geeky partner, with as much dignity as he could muster, removed the thong from its perch and dropped it on the table on his way to the bed.

He said not a word.

He did not once glance her way.

He crawled under the covers and ignored her.

Miffed at his reaction, Valaska—mostly—ignored him back.

What was it about Dex that intrigued her? It wasn't as if he turned her on with his prowess. She'd never met a clumsier male, or a more awkward one.

Yet, he wasn't awkward when he was in scientist mode. The intelligence and assurance he'd displayed proved attractive.

Which made no sense.

Amazons prized males for their virility. Strong men made strong babies. Thing was they weren't much fun to talk to. Apart from a handful—who annoyingly enough had wives or partners—she rarely met a man who not only boasted physical strength but also a modicum of intelligence. Or at least enough wits to verbally spar with her.

While she might tease Adexios about the fact he liked to read, the truth was she read in secret too. Secret because her friends would make fun.

She knew what Luddite meant, and she'd spotted all the same things he had when they came across the puddles, but she didn't mention it aloud. Why not? Of all people, he was the least likely to make fun of her for geeking out, and yet a lifetime spent pretending she was just a dumb warrior stuck.

She liked it that way. It gave her the element of surprise, and that, in turn, helped her win more fights.

But Adexios isn't a fight. He's a man. A wiry, smart, very well-endowed man who was like nobody she'd ever met.

He was also the only man to not try and seduce her when she made her intentions clear. The only man to not toss her on a table and give her five minutes of fun. The only man to treat her with respect.

What a jerk.

What a challenge.

I'll teach you to ignore me.

Chapter Eight

"Distraction and dereliction might earn points with Lucifer, but on the Styx, it could get you swallowed and digested for centuries." As preached by his father the first time Adexios got eaten by a sea beast while reading a book.

Why is she so hard to ignore?

The question plagued Adexios as he feigned sleep in the extremely comfortable bed, more comfortable than his own, he should add. He would really have to think about perhaps breaking the lease on his apartment and finding a permanent spot to park his cabin once this was all over.

If he survived. And by survived he didn't mean the mission. He meant the torture of being around Valaska.

The woman was crazy. Utterly fearless. Absolutely splendid, and scarier than the fucking abyss.

She teased him at every turn, had even invited him to take a taste. Yet, he couldn't. Wouldn't. Not because he didn't want to. *I definitely want her.* But because he feared what would happen if he did.

He couldn't shake a nagging belief that an erotic moment with her would ruin him for all others. A foolish thought with absolutely no basis. He'd had sex before and knew it felt good. But given his intense attraction to Valaska, he could almost predict sex with her would scream past good to mind-blowing.

And his mind was the only thing he had going for him.

Given his restlessness, which he didn't understand since his body was quite tired, he fell back on a trick he'd used as a child to relax himself. He counted things.

One. One stupid mission.

Two. Two days since he'd met her.

Three. Three minutes since he'd crawled into bed.

Four. Four-eyed geek who kicked ass—at Scrabble.

Five. Five fingers to jerk off with. Or was that four because of his thumb.

Six. Six skip ahead to nine because, combined, that led to lots of fun.

Back to seven. Seven thrusts to make him come.

Eight. Eight fucking hours until dawn.

Nine. Hanging with six still being sixty-nines were fun for everyone.

Ten. Ten could fuck itself. This wasn't working. He was now officially even more wound up than before. Hyperawareness sucked, especially if you wanted to get out of bed and find a snack.

Except he didn't know what Valaska was doing. He'd taken the bed, leaving her the couch—again, showing his support of women's lib and treating her like an equal. Despite listening intently, he'd not heard the groan of furniture as she lay upon it. He'd not heard a damned thing since he stalked off to bed.

What is she up to?

The cabin proved awfully quiet. Was Valaska even here, or had she returned outside to play with the insect life?

He dared a peek. Since he'd placed his glasses on

the nightstand, his vision saw the world in bleary smudges. He spotted nothing to his left but the wall to the bathroom. Quietly, he shifted onto his back, but the view of the timbered ceiling did nothing for him. Especially since the fact that he was myopically challenged meant all he saw was a big brown blob.

He rolled over to his right and…

Screamed. "What the fuck!"

A rapier gaze observed him without blinking. Crouched beside his bed, Valaska let a smile curve her lips. "Hello, Dex."

"Don't you hello me, brat. You just scared at least a century off my life. What are you doing sneaking up on me?"

"Not sneaking, merely changing locations because the couch is too short for me."

"And?" He played deliberately obtuse to hide the fact that his heart had started beating faster.

"This bed is pretty big."

"And?" He knew she wanted an invitation to join him. But he couldn't. Just couldn't.

"Move over."

"What happened to roughing it?"

"You want me to get rough?" Even without his glasses, he caught the mischievous glint. Before he could roll away, she'd pounced on him.

"Get off me," he gasped.

"Is this your way of telling me I am too heavy?" Her lips hovered only a hairsbreadth away.

"No, this is my way of saying your knee is uncomfortably close to my manparts."

She grinned. "I know. It's intentional because you called me a brat. Care to say it again?"

Hmm. Say it once and she was straddling him. Say it twice and… Perhaps she'd start removing layers so they could touch skin-to-skin.

Shudder. *I should be so lucky.*

She mistook his shiver for something else. "Do I frighten you, Dex?"

Honestly? "Yeah."

"And yet"—she squirmed atop him and he couldn't help the moan that escaped—"you desire me."

No use denying it. "You are attractive."

Her smile widened. "I think you're cute, too."

She did? That flustered him. "Cute, but so obviously not your type."

"Exactly what is my type?"

Try anybody but him? "A guy who can hold his own in battle, who isn't scared of a fight." *And who has the courage to seduce you.*

"I don't know. That does seem to describe you. You didn't leave me to battle the wasp alone. You came to my rescue."

"With killer cologne."

"Was the bug any less dead?" she asked with an arched brow.

"You could probably kick my ass in a fight."

"Yes. I could. But don't feel bad. I could kick most men's asses in a fight." She shrugged. "It's part of being who I am. It doesn't mean I can't find you attractive."

"You think I'm attractive?" He really wished he possessed a deeper baritone and didn't sound so surprised.

"Very. I'll bet you're a beast in bed."

"I don't shapeshift during sex."

She laughed. "I meant you are probably an intense lover. And a believer in foreplay obviously, given your slow seduction of me."

"What are you talking about? I haven't tried to

seduce you." Did she mistake for someone else? *Tell me who and I'll take them for a ride down the river Styx, a journey they won't return from.*

"Are you sure of that? I mean you did, after all, manage to entice me into bed. You have me wet with anticipation. And your cock is obviously ready for action."

He'd enticed her? "I think—"

"The problem is you think too much," she muttered before silencing his protests with her lips.

Did she really think she could control him and force him to her way of thinking by using her feminine wiles on him?

Damn her for knowing his weakness. He totally crumbled at the first touch. Why was he still fighting her? She wanted him. He wanted her. What else did he need to know?

How does she feel? And he wasn't exactly referring to her emotions. His fingertips longed to trace her shape and learn every nuance of her body.

As her lips slid across his with sensual exploration, his hands emerged from under the blankets to stroke the bared skin of her back.

Unlike other girls he'd slept with, Valaska didn't have smooth flesh. Instead, his fingers stroked over hard ridges, scar tissue from battle. He felt the toned muscle of a warrior who kept herself fit. He caressed the body of a woman, a woman not afraid to experience life to its fullest.

And now she wanted to experience him.

A chest-thumping moment for a guy like him.

A fearful rabbit-foot-thumping moment as well.

There were probably many reasons he should stop what they did. So many cons, starting with the fact that they worked together.

Big no-no. The Association for Ferryman employee handbook had a whole chapter devoted to rule number six, which was don't fraternize, cannibalize, patricide, or theorize while on the job.

But breaking the rules at work means earning points with the big guy.

Quick, think of another negative.

How about their general incompatibility with one another? She liked to kill things for fun. He did, too, but on his video game console. He wore boxers; she wore thongs. A choice he could totally live with.

Although, right now, she's not wearing anything, according to his roaming hands. He cupped her full, bare bottom and groaned.

What negatives was he thinking of? There were no cons in the here and now. He couldn't see any problem with what was happening within the dimly lit cabin, in a feather-filled bed. The only negative left was the fact that a stupid quilted comforter separated their naked bodies.

A minor detail. For the moment, he contented himself with the taste of her lips and embracing her tongue when it insinuated itself between his lips.

She groaned, the sound so surprising he paused in their kiss.

"Why are you stopping?" She raised her head, her lips full and swollen, her eyelids heavy with lust. Lust for him.

"You really do want me." He said it with a note of wonderment.

A smile curved her mouth. Extending her arms, she arched herself over him, and he would have wondered why except the turgid peak of her nipple stabbed at him.

He didn't need her growled, "Suck it," to know

what was expected. He latched onto that bud with the hunger of a man deprived.

With his lips, he tugged the tight bud, sucking and pulling it into his mouth. He felt the quiver that went through her body. A long shudder that he caused.

As he continued to tease the tip of her breast, he slid his hand down the side of her ribcage, past the indent of her waist, then far enough to stroke the shaven skin of her mound.

Again, she shivered, and she hissed, "Yes. Touch me." Her hips lifted enough for him to slide his hand between her thighs.

The wetness of her sex immediately honeyed his fingers. His turn to moan, the rumble vibrating against the breast he held in his mouth. He found himself somewhat distracted as he let his digits circle her warm, swollen flesh.

He slid one finger in. Hot. Wet. Pulsing decadence.

Another finger, not enough to really stretch her much yet. And she would need to stretch to take his cock. In went a third finger, tightening the fit, the muscles of her channel clenching him tight.

That was enough fingers for now. He pumped them within her heated core, feeling the quiver as her excitement built.

"Yes. Yes." Her hips gyrated in time to his thrusts, pulling his fingers as deep as they could go. Should he add a fourth one?

Fuck asking. He thrust it in. A sharp cry left her, as he now had to push his thicker offering into her sex.

Faster he pumped. Faster she bounced.

Her breathing quickened, and he couldn't help but peek at her, arched above him, hand gripping the headboard, her breasts swaying in time to their motions, her eyes closed, her lips parted.

She was an utter goddess.

He growled. "Look at me." She moaned. "Look at me. I want to see you when you come."

Obeying him, she opened her eyes and gazed down at him, her expression soft and glazed, the look of a woman in the throes of passion. A woman who uttered soft, mewling cries as he pounded his fingers in.

With his free hand, he tweaked a nipple, twisting the tight bud.

Her sex clamped down tight around his fingers. Her mouth opened wide. Her eyes lost focus.

She came hard, a strident scream leaving her lips, the muscles of her channel pulsing and gripping his still-pumping fingers.

"That's it, baby. Come for me." The dirty words flowed from his lips, words he'd never dared utter to anyone else.

"Oh fuck. Oh fuck." She chanted it over and over as she continued to ride his fingers, her first orgasm dying but her pleasure still at a peak.

"Are you ready for my cock, baby?" he asked. His cock certainly was. It throbbed. It pushed at the offending blankets that dared separate him from her heated splendor.

"Oh. Oh," she panted. "Is it me, or is the whole place shaking?"

Was there anything more awesome for a guy who'd pleasured his woman to hear than the fact that he made her whole world rock?

Except, in this case, it wasn't the wicked orgasm that was the cause.

"Holy fuck, hellquake!"

Chapter Nine

"If at first you don't succeed, chop off its head."
From the Amazon Guide to the Undead Apocalypse.

As the whole house trembled—almost as much as her body still did—Valaska leaped off her surprisingly skilled lover and stood on the vibrating floor.

The shaking proved intense. "W-w-ill the c-c-abin h-h-old?" Her words stuttered as the cabin continued to rattle.

"M-may-b-b-e," Dex replied as he rolled out of the bed, his shaft projecting thickly from his groin. Apparently it hadn't received the message yet that they were in danger.

As the house continued to vibrate, Valaska decided it might be best to prepare herself. While battling naked didn't bother her, breasts flying about could prove a hazard, especially when they got in the way of a sword thrust.

At least she wasn't too well endowed in that area, not like poor Nespa, who needed to keep them bound on training runs lest she knock herself out.

"How long is this going to last?" Dex shouted as he dove into his own clothes.

She didn't answer immediately due to her entertainment as she watched him try to stuff his hard cock into his pants. His cock really wasn't on board with that plan and kept springing back out.

"Usually hellquakes last a few seconds to a few

minutes." While they didn't happen often, these tremors did occur, with varying degrees of violence, and didn't cause much harm, unless a person happened to be in a home or building that collapsed when it happened. Even outhouses weren't safe. Poor Mona had found that out the gross way.

The trembling reached a pitch. The whole house gave a big lurch, enough to stagger her.

To her surprise, Adexios kept his footing.

At her surely shocked look, he smiled. "Sea legs. I'm used to Styx monsters trying to tip my boat."

The intense vibration stopped, and yet…something wasn't right.

"Is it me or does it feel like we're moving?" she asked. More like subtly rocking.

His brows pulled into a frown. "Yeah, it does seem that way. Reminds me of the motion of a boat."

At his words, she ran to the window, vaulting over the couch to reach it faster. Speed didn't change what she saw.

"We're afloat!"

Indeed the cabin, ripped from its perch, currently bobbed along a dark current. Where had all the water come from? It hadn't rained, and they'd not camped near any of the larger puddles.

Coming to stand beside her, Adexios peeked out. "Looks like the puddle situation has gotten worse."

"You think!" She strapped on the rest of her gear, grabbed her spear, and went to the door. Flinging it open, she regarded the fast-flowing water.

Dex grabbed her by the arm and pulled her away from the opening. "What are you doing?"

"Jumping ship, or is that cabin? Whatever. I'm getting out of here."

"Are you insane?"

"I thought we already discussed that."

He rolled his eyes. "Sorry, I meant to say, are you suicidal? Take a look out there." He flicked a switch, and an outdoor light came on over the door.

The one dim bulb didn't illuminate far, but it showed enough. As far as she could see, water. Water. And more water. Not the still water of the little puddles they'd encountered. Not the clear depths where she could see the bottom.

This liquid bore the appearance of a storm-tossed sea. Dark waves, with a strong briny stench. White caps crested and rolled, their strength carrying the cabin along to who knew where.

If she jumped out in that, loaded with all her gear, she'd probably sink. Swimming wasn't high on her list of strong suits, even if she rocked a bikini.

"I'm going to assume you can't breath underwater?" he remarked.

"No, but I can hold my breath pretty damned long. Drop your pants and I'll show you."

Yes, she was intentionally blatant in order to distract attention from the fact that she was seriously discomfited by their situation. Being at the mercy of her environment didn't sit well. She liked to be able to kill, or at least seriously maim, the things that bothered her.

Just in case... She poked the sea water with her spear. A nice hard jab.

It didn't scream.

Damn.

"I don't suppose you think it's shallow enough to wade in?"

He cast a dubious gaze. "Doubt it."

She pushed her spear down into the rolling waves. Down. And down some more. She stopped pushing when the tips of her fingers got wet.

"Pretty deep," she remarked, followed by a, "What the fuck!" as her spear was torn from her grasp.

"Strong current," he remarked.

"That didn't feel like any current," she said with a glare at the dark water that mocked her.

"They're stronger than you think."

For some reason, his words had her eyeing him. "Yes, they are," she muttered.

Funny, how his chest thrust out at the same time as his cheeks took on a bit of color.

He studiously avoided her gaze as he kept staring out the door. "With it still being dark, and us not knowing how far or bad the water situation has gotten—"

"I'll go on a limb and say fairly dire."

"—we are both better off staying inside and waiting to see what happens. Perhaps once the dawn hits, we'll be better able to strategize and extricate ourselves from this situation."

"You mean you want us to do…" She took a moment to make a face before saying the dreaded word. "Nothing?" Sitting still wasn't her strong suit. She hated being idle. "Fuck me," she muttered.

"Maybe later if you're *good.*"

Um, who'd said that? She cast a startled glance at Dex, but he wasn't paying her any attention. Maybe she'd misheard. Maybe the devil was playing tricks.

Or maybe Dex was a slyer player than she gave him credit for because there it was, a hint of mischief tugging at his lips.

Sexy.

Almost as sexy as the fact that he didn't cower at their situation but logically analyzed it.

He knelt by the doorframe. Water lapped at the edge, and yet some kind of odd magic kept it from slopping in.

A good thing or she might find herself a touch worried about sinking.

Bracing one hand on the floor, Dex shoved the other one into the water.

"What are you doing? Trying to get your hand chewed off by some aquatic monster?"

"Sea monsters don't chew. They rip limbs off."

"Either way, you're like a wiggly worm on a pole, very tempting."

"Did you truly compare me to a wiggly worm?" He looked and sounded so pained.

She couldn't help but laugh. "Sorry, should I have said thick python?"

"Thick and long, thank you."

That retort earned a belly laugh from her. Through her snorts and guffaws, she managed to gasp, "Dex, you hide the most evil sense of humor."

"Thank you."

"No, thank you, for not making this mission totally suck."

"Thanks again, I think."

Did he not grasp the compliment she paid him? Amazon warriors did not partner with men, especially those who couldn't bench-press a hellcat—which, for the uninformed, somehow weighed more than a car. Her kind didn't have long conversations with men, and they certainly didn't laugh with them. Laugh at yes, but with? Her geeky companion was a rare treat.

I should keep him once this is over.

Slap.

Get a hold of yourself. Only the truly mentally deranged—who'd gotten smacked one too many times in the noggin obviously—settled down with a man.

Not me. She intended to follow the pure Amazon

way. Fuck 'em and leave 'em. Or kill 'em. Whichever proved most practical.

Time to get her head back into the game, starting with, "Why are you sticking your hand in the water if not for bait?"

"I'm checking on things."

"Like what? Whether we'll expire of hypothermia or drown first? I'm going to state right now that neither is high on my list."

He cast her an amused stare. "What happened to death being glorious during the course of adventure?"

"That was if it happened during battle. This"— she pointed at the icky waves—"has no honor."

"Then I guess we'll have to make sure we don't die."

She liked his optimism. *Live that we might kill another day.*

A sudden burst of song erupted. The tune for 'Number of the Beast' by Twisted Sister belted, and, yes, she happened to know that song as she'd gone through a heavy metal phase in her teens.

"That's my phone," he stated as he dug in his pocket for it. "It's the devil," he stated unnecessarily with a roll of his eyes.

But despite his irritation at the interruption, he answered and put the caller on speakerphone. He placed the hellphone on the floor beside him as he continued to lean out the door to study the water situation.

"Hey, boss. Can you call back later? I'm kind of busy right now."

"Busy? Really?" Lucifer sounded pleased. "Why you old lint ball off your father's robe. You move quicker than expected, son. I am so proud of you. Debauching that Amazon chick the first night out."

"I didn't exactly debauch."

She snickered and whispered, "Yeah, you did."

How his eyes gleamed behind his glasses. "Wait until later," he mouthed.

My, my but she quite enjoyed the many facets to her geek.

"Aha, I knew you did something, boy. The devil always knows. So tell me, is she a screamer?"

"A gentleman never tells. And for the record, the ravishment of my lady companion is not the reason I'm busy. We're kind of in mortal peril."

"So you didn't stick it to her?" Lucifer sounded so disappointed.

"What Valaska and I may or may not have done is none of your business. I need you to focus, as this is important. The puddle situation has gotten critical."

"Yes, so I heard. I had to summon a protective ring around the ninth circle to keep that damned water from flooding Hell."

"And you didn't think to send us help?"

"I called, didn't I?"

"The great lord's care for his minions is without reproach," Valaska chimed in.

"Ass-kisser," Dex muttered.

"If you insist, but I'd prefer to leave my teeth marks in your buttocks," she sassed back.

"Are you two done flirting with each other? Because it's annoying, unless you're planning to get naked, in which case, I'll just listen and find out for myself if she screams."

"We are not getting naked. But we are currently afloat on an ocean that didn't exist a few hours ago."

"Ah, yes, that pesky sea water that has appeared. What in all that is mighty—which is me of course—is going on?"

"Damned if I know what's happening," Dex said,

looking right at her.

Good, she liked to keep a man on his toes.

Thankfully, Lucifer was oblivious to the undertones. "You're already damned, Adexios. I want answers. You know how I feel about people who fail me."

"You reward them for not living up to their full potential."

"Well, yes, I do, but that is…" the devil blustered. "Stop screwing with me, boy, or I'll have you mucking out the latrines for a few centuries. I want answers."

Threatened or not, her geek remain undaunted.

Dex's lips curled, a mischievous boy about to yank the tail on the devil. "Aren't we all looking for answers, though? Such as how do they get the gooey caramel center into a Caramilk bar? And why is it, whenever I wear white jeans, I sit in something sticky."

"Probably because men should never wear white jeans." Valaska shook her head. "Ever."

"They don't start out white," he muttered. "I have issues with bleach."

She blew a rude noise. "Real men don't use bleach either."

How cute he looked when he got all flustered. Agitated, he pushed his glasses up his nose. "Forget about the bleach. The point I was getting at is that sometimes things like delicious treats and suddenly appearing seas don't have an answer."

"Okay," said Lucifer.

Dex waited, but nothing more appeared forthcoming. "That's it? Okay?"

The devil snorted. "Yeah, okay. I'm not stupid, boy. I know that when you're dealing with omnipotent deities like me, shit happens. Weird shit most of the time."

Valaska jumped on Lucifer's words. "You think this new sea is the result of some other god screwing in your realm?"

"Someone is playing in Lucifer's sandbox? No way. I thought you were the toughest dude around." Dex breathed the words in feigned shock. Thing was, the devil couldn't see his face so he didn't know Dex teased.

Lucifer uttered a big growling noise. "No one fucks with me."

"Hate to break it to you, boss, but someone is."

A deep sigh came through the phone. "People are always trying to come after my power. Isn't it grand? Always some new calamity coming along to keep a handsome devil in tiptop shape."

"This is more than a calamity. You'd better invest in life rafts then. I have a feeling they're going to sell out in a little bit because, unless we find the source to this water and stop it, I'm going to go on record and say I think we're all going to get wet."

Speaking of wet, Valaska couldn't help but snicker and mutter. "Get us out of this alive, Dex, and I promise to soak you."

There was that lovely blush she wanted—*I wonder how far down his body it extends.*

As he gaped at her, they could hear Lucifer bellow.

"Stop this flood from happening, Adexios. Just because my brother thought it was a good idea to do it on the mortal plane when mankind wouldn't toe his line doesn't mean I need it happening in the pit."

"Maybe God will let you borrow that Noah fellow to build an ark."

"I am not asking that cheap do-gooder for anything. Because you are going to fix this. And as incentive, once this is over, you can have whatever job you want."

"Fix this he says. Is that all?"

"Fix it now, or I'll roast your ribs for dinner!" Lucifer bellowed. They heard a clatter, probably the phone as it went for a ride, but although it landed hard, it didn't hang up.

"Gaia! Wench, where are you hiding now? I need my slicker and my rubber boots."

"Not the horned duckies again." They could hear Gaia sigh. "Can't you wear something a little more your age?"

An indignant Lucifer huffed before he replied, "Are you mocking my outfit, woman?"

"Yes. Yes I am. Care to *punish* me?"

"Wait until I catch you, wench."

Midway through Mother Nature's squealing giggle, Dex hung up. "I don't think we need to hear out what happens next."

"Why listen when we could make noises of our own?" While he did get a pink hint to his cheeks, he didn't immediately pounce on her to start making music.

Instead he said, "What should we do now?"

Given they were stuck in the cabin for the moment, her first thought was to go back to bed and finish what they'd started. However, that was the weak womanly side of her talking, the same side that thought they should keep Dex and play house.

Ugh.

The Amazon warrior knew what had to be done instead.

Stand guard and watch, as well as, "Wait and see where the tide takes us."

Chapter Ten

"Don't feed the Styx Monsters. They're spoiled enough as it is." An often heard rant of Charon's.

As dawn lightened the sky, the fingertips of a reddish radiance poking at his closed eyelids, Adexios stretched then froze.

I think I'm using someone's lap as a pillow.

While he might have initially fallen asleep sitting alongside Valaska, somehow during the course of his slumber, he'd slumped over and now found his head pillowed on her thighs.

"About time you woke," she grumbled, yet she did so good-naturedly.

"How long was I out?" he asked, staying where he was. A smart man, he was in no hurry to move.

"A few hours."

"Did you get any sleep?"

"Some."

He peeled open an eyelid and glanced at her. Judging by her rigid body and the way she kept staring out the open door, he doubted what sleep she'd gotten amounted to much.

Since she also seemed in no hurry to move, he continued talking. "How's it looking outside?"

She grimaced. "Wet."

"Really?" He turned his face to the side, toward her, not away. His lips hovered over the juncture of her thighs. Only the leather of her bottoms separated him from her sex. "How wet?" He blew hotly and couldn't help a spurt of manly satisfaction when a quiver went through her.

"While your concern with my satisfaction is appreciated, I believe we have more pressing matters."

"Nothing more pressing than this," he murmured, on a brazen streak. He pressed his mouth against the seam of her shorts.

Her breath drew in with a sharp gasp.

"Dex!"

"I like it when you say my name like that," he growled against her.

"Dex, behind you!"

He rolled off her lap as Valaska sprang to her feet. In but a moment, she stood in a ready stance with her sword in hand.

Getting to his knees, Adexios peeked at the doorway to see what had her yelling.

One giant eyeball, suspended on a purple, slimy stalk wavered outside the door.

"Well, hello there, Mr. Sea Monster," Adexios said as he rose slowly. "I don't believe we've met before."

The massive orb blinked.

"I don't suppose you know where you came from?"

A long blink.

"Are you seriously talking to it?" she hissed. "We should kill it now before it calls its friends."

"Not everything needs to die," he replied, taking a careful step forward. He held his hands out at the side, empty of weapons as he tried to soothe their visitor. "Nice sea monster. My name is Adexios. Would you like a treat?"

Valaska snorted. "Sure it would. A treat

comprised of a yummy idiot who is talking instead of chopping up our visitor for a sushi breakfast."

"Watch and learn." He rummaged in his pocket and pulled out half a chocolate bar. Adexios waved it in front of him, noting how the eyeball tracked his movements.

"How's he supposed to eat that?" she asked with clear confusion. "Oh."

A tentacle rose from the bumpy waves and snatched the offering. It disappeared back into the water.

The creature blinked. Blinked again. If it was possible for a giant eyeball to smile, this one did.

A horn sounded, but a horn unlike any he'd ever heard before. A long, low, bass sound that made Adexios' teeth vibrate and the hair on his arms rise.

The giant eye turned to look off into the distance. Without even a blink goodbye, it sank under the waves.

Never a good sign when the monsters ran away.

"What the fuck now?" Valaska asked.

Adexios had an inkling that turned into a nagging certainty when the sound of the horn faded and a strong breeze started.

This definitely is not good.

"We might be in a spot of trouble."

"Trouble how?"

"I think I know that horn. Or at least I know of it."

"So what does it mean? Or do I need to torture the answer out of you?"

A part of him was tempted to see what type of torture she'd employ. Erotic torture especially intrigued. However, the situation really was rather dire.

"A big monster is coming."

"Really?" Rather than cower, her posture

straightened.

"Yes, really. Ever heard of a kraken?"

"Yes." Her eyes shone, and she wet her lips.

"If I'm correct, the horn sound we heard is the one used to call them."

She didn't question how the kraken, like that other sea monster, had arrived in this sea, hadn't existed the day before. Instead, she focused on the important part. "How much time before it arrives?"

Given the summons was magical, and their need to answer if they heard the call imperative? "Now."

As if he'd practiced the timing, a brown tentacle shot out of the wave nearest the door and, in sea monsters' language, waved, "Hello, land dweller, prepare to die."

Before he could yell—because yelling seemed like the right thing to do when confronted by one of the deadliest creatures in the sea—Valaska darted forward and swung. The sharp edge of her blade severed the slimy appendage, with an ease much like his mother's when she sliced through the crowd during the annual Hellmart clearance sale.

The squirming tip, with its perilous suckers, fell—on the floor inside the cabin!

Adexios darted out of the way, careful to not touch it. "Watch out for those spikes in the center of the suction cups. They're laced with a narcotic that causes paralysis in the kraken's prey."

"Seriously? A giant monster that could crush me in its grip, probably eat me in one bite, and who outweighs me several dozen times over, also has poison?"

"Yes."

"Awesome. I love a challenge."

And he loved her fierce bravery. However, it was

stupidity that he needed to guard her against. "Not awesome. Like crazy dangerous."

"Yes."

"As in you-could-die dangerous," he expanded.

"Yes."

"Will anything I say deter you from fighting it?"

She didn't even pretend to think about it. "No."

He sighed. "Very well, then if you insist, you should know a few things about the kraken. I've already mentioned the poison. It goes without saying that you should avoid it, unless you don't mind getting eaten and digested over the course of a few years."

"Don't get eaten. Check." She took a moment to strap a knife to her ankle.

"When the kraken's body emerges from the waves, you'll note it has a squid-like head, a giant mouth lined in very sharp teeth and one enormous eye."

"Sounds like an easy target." Her smile turned upside down in disappointment.

That was about to change. "No, it's not that easy, seeing as how the eye is a camouflage feature. Most people go for it, thinking they'll blind or kill the kraken. But taking out the eye does nothing. The suckers on the tentacles"—he kicked at the still-twitching limb until it rolled out the door—"act as some kind of visual receptor. It's how it can see and aim for its prey, even if the body is still under water."

"Damn, that's some awesome defense systems. How do you know this?" she asked casually before lunging at the door and, with a rapid slash back and forth, decapitated two more questing tentacles.

"I took Hell's version of marine biology in university."

"You went on to get a higher education when you graduated? I thought that was reserved as a punishment for those who slacked at school in their mortal life?"

"What can I say? I'm a masochist for learning. My mother was mortified, especially when I finished top of my class. But on the upside, I now know everything there is to know about the different classes of sea monsters and how to handle them."

"Speaking of handle, hold this for a second." She thrust her sword at him.

His fingers gripped the pommel of the lightweight blade. He held it out in front of him gingerly, somewhat worried he might drop it and impale his foot. He'd done that once with Neptune's trident when the sea god came to dinner at his parents' house. "What am I supposed to do with this?"

"Whack off anything that comes through that door."

"Me? I'm supposed to be the brains of this operation. You're the brawn." And he felt no shame in pointing out the obvious. "What will you be doing if I'm defending us?"

"Lightening the load."

And by lightening, she meant stripping. Off came her top, revealing her breasts in all their splendor. High, firm, and topped with a dark red berry.

A wiggly tentacle came through the door and zinged toward her, aiming for those breasts.

Mine! He couldn't have said if he shouted the thought in his mind or aloud. He did, however, slash at the offending kraken limb. It hit the floor with a wet thump while the wagging stump spewed some neon-green gore.

Eew.

Without missing a beast, Valaska sidestepped the jetting ichor while, at the same time, kicking off her boots. She then shoved down her shorts, which left her clad only in her skimpy underwear. She also wore his ardent gaze, but that didn't do much to cover the amount of tempting skin on display.

He thought she might be done with her tease.

Nope.

There went the thong. This time he didn't bother removing it from the frame of his glasses, where it dangled. Why remove it when he rather enjoyed smelling the lingering traces of Valaska's passion. A pity there would not be a repeat, seeing as how she was determined to kill herself.

"You're going to go fight the kraken naked?" he observed.

"Not entirely." She pointed to her ankle with its strapped knife.

"You could have kept the panties," he remarked, distracted by the appearance of her bare mound. He didn't have the manners or strength to look away.

"You are such a prude, Dex. Tell you what, how about next time there's the possibility I'll fight a sea monster, I make sure I bring a bikini?"

"That works for me."

She rolled her eyes. "Give me back my sword."

With pleasure. She took it from him, and just in time. She leaped in the air just as a tentacle came whipping through the door, looking to trip her.

Adexios jumped back, making sure to stay far away. He didn't have a weapon to fight with. Not even a paddle.

But the fireplace did have a poker. Grabbing the heavy metal rod, he was just in time to see the severed stump slide back out the open door, disappearing under the waves. As to the remaining bit that oozed on the floor, Valaska tapped her chin. "I wonder how kraken tentacle tastes breaded and deep fried."

Maybe he'd toss a chunk in the interdimensional pocket that led to his mom's fridge. If anyone knew how to cook kraken, it was her. "Can we discuss recipes later? I think you just pissed the kraken off."

Indeed, the water outside the cabin churned, and their tiny makeshift ship was tossed. If not for the effort of the valiant two, their cabin would be lost.

Funny, how he suddenly had an urge to watch *Gilligan's Island.*

"If I don't make it back," she said, "be sure to tell my sisters I died with extreme honor."

Died? No. She couldn't.

Valaska smothered any protest he might have uttered by plastering him with a kiss. A kiss full of passion. A kiss full of hunger. A kiss for him.

Then, she was gone, sword in hand, diving into the waves, even as the massive body of the kraken crested.

Ominous music played in his head.

For a moment, Adexios stared at the massive beast. It was one thing to see drawings, and read about the monsters, another to truly encounter one.

On the Styx, the sea monsters were big but, for the most part, fairly harmless, at least to him. His dad had an understanding with the beasts along the lines of *Try to eat me and my family and I will turn this into another Dead Sea.* No one ever discussed that ill-fated vacation his parents had taken that resulted in his dad having a bit of a temper tantrum.

Whatever happened, word spread, and the monsters in the river behaved, except for the mischief they indulged in with Adexios.

However, the kraken didn't live in the river that flowed through hell. The kraken were true oceanic predators, living deep below the dark waves, in caverns where they hid until called.

But the question was, who'd called it?

Adexios scanned the waves, looking for a boat of some kind, anything that would show where the person was who had sounded the horn.

All Adexios could see was the barnacle-covered, mutant-appearing, octopus-based kraken. It really was an ugly beast with its bulbous eye, the iris comprised of pure black. Its giant mouth gaped, and as it exhaled, it emitted an obnoxious sound, part foghorn, part chittering with a breath that was definitely fetid.

Ugh. "A little oral hygiene wouldn't hurt," he muttered.

Humor at a time like this? It was better than worrying about Valaska, who'd yet to reappear since her dive and to whom, he'd just realized, he'd not told the secret to killing the kraken.

She doesn't know its heart and brain are in its belly.

Shit. Not that the knowledge would make the task any easier.

Kraken were notoriously hard to kill—at least they had been in the old days. In today's modern world, science now had ways of evening the odds, if you had the right connections, which Adexios did. What a proud moment for his mother when she'd realized he was wheeling and dealing for illegal goods on Hell's underground white market.

He scrambled for his pack.

"I know they're in here somewhere." He'd packed them; he was sure he had. Not that he'd expected to use his special buys on kraken. When he'd bought the incredibly potent hand grenades he'd been thinking more along the lines of using them to take out any giant swamp monsters they encountered.

Who cared why he'd bought them? He at least had some. Adexios grabbed all five explosive spheres, hoping they would prove enough.

Because where there was one kraken, there were usually more.

Chapter Eleven

"Always keep your two feet on the ground when fighting unless you're riding a dragon. Then land first before you kill it." An Amazon rule inspired by Sophie's Splat.

A beautiful day for a swim and some fishing, Valaska thought as she dove with glee into the water.

The water wasn't as cold as she expected, and yet it still hit her system with a shock. It definitely erased any lingering passionate heat.

On the plus side as well, Valaska didn't immediately sink. The sword, even though lightweight, however, pulled her arm down. She had to work harder in waves to compensate for it. The salt water provided some buoyancy, along with her scissoring feet. With a bit of effort, she managed to keep moving in a horizontal direction.

While the light somewhat penetrated the medium she swam through, the water itself proved a touch murky, no longer sporting the crystal clarity they'd noted in the puddles.

Despite the reduced visibility, she still managed to note the flailing tentacles of the kraken. A beast she knew very little about. *Although I know more now, thanks to Dex.*

Don't aim for the eye. Good to know, except with the eye taken out of the equation, she didn't know what she should aim for.

"Fuck!" The expletive left her in bubbles that floated to the surface. Speaking of which, she kicked up and hauled in a quick breath before popping back down.

The closer she got to the beast, the more careful she had to be. This was its playground. The kraken was quite at home in the water, whereas Valaska hated battles where her feet didn't touch the ground.

It meant there was a lot less force behind her swings.

Stupid sword was less than useless under the water. But she did love it. It was a gift from a dying viper demon in a battle over a decade ago. She'd taken it from his clutching fingers, even as she delivered the killing blow.

Good times.

However, as much as she loved the sword, it was useless in this situation. Back to the surface she kicked, hard and fast, propelling herself much like a missile until she burst the watery skin and, in a smooth motion, learned in training, fired her sword at the bobbing cabin.

The tip of her blade hit the log exterior with a *thunk* that embedded it and left it quivering.

She had time to yell, "The water's great!" to a gaping Dex before slipping back down under the waves.

She palmed her knife, razor sharp and much easier to stab and slice with. The only problem was that, each time she scored a hit on a tentacle, the water grew murkier and murkier. Stupid kraken was bleeding like crazy; it just wasn't dying.

The limbs were in a frenzy, the good news being, the less she could see, the less those sucker-type eyes could too. Hacking at the tentacles, though, wouldn't get the job done. She needed to find its weak spot.

She aimed herself for the big body, narrowly escaping the grasp of a tentacle, the whip of it so close she felt the slime of its skin. She reached the bulky body of the kraken, its skin mottled with bumps. Also known as handholds for the intrepid.

Clasping her dagger in her mouth, Valaska grasped at the nodules, using them to climb the side of the beast, pulling herself upward, past the water line into the air and the hell light illuminating the churning sea.

She heard Adexios bellow, "Fire in the hole!"

Casting a glance sideways, she caught him winding back and tossing a glass sphere right into the maw of the beast.

She scrambled faster as Dex screamed, "She's gonna blow. Jump off."

"I'm going as fast as I can," she muttered around the blade she clutched with her teeth. It didn't help that she had to dodge flailing appendages. But she did it.

She leaped onto the head of the sea monster just as a shudder went through it. Taking a run atop the bulbous surface, she tossed her knife and then leaped, just as the beast uttered a high-pitched squeal.

While the aerial push from the explosion was welcome in propelling her a few extra feet so that she landed on the roof of the cabin with a hard thump, the chunks of kraken raining down on her weren't as welcome, especially since they oozed in some places and steamed in others.

"Valaska!" Dex yelled. "Valaska, are you all right?"

Crawling across the pitching deck of the roof, she leaned over the edge and yelled, "Boo!"

He screamed. Then cursed. "Don't fucking do that!"

"You killed the monster, Dex. I am so jealous. Wait until I tell my tribe."

"I blew it up. No big deal."

He claimed nonchalance, but she could see the pleasure in his expression at her praise.

"I'm glad it's not a big deal because here come more of them."

Given he couldn't see as well as she could from his vantage, she offered him a hand. However, he eschewed her aid and, displaying an agility she suspected he purposely hid, soon joined her on the roof.

"Where are they?" he asked, a useless question, given the water churning around them. Two more spots.

"How many more bombs do you have?"

He dug into his pockets before he held a pair out in each hand. "Four, but I was lucky with the one I just tossed. The kraken was close enough even I couldn't miss."

Good point. The other two emerging sea monsters hadn't surfaced as closely.

"Give me a pair," she ordered.

"What are you planning to do?" he asked.

"Sushi bomb!"

Her plan was simple. Swim to the kraken and toss the bomb in its mouth.

Easy? At least once she'd battled past the tentacles, managed to bob above the waves in front of it, and tossed it in. It was the disorientation once the kraken blew that troubled her.

With the first one she blew into chunks, she lucked out and ended up fairly close to her second target. Problem was she was getting tired, and a tentacle managed a little scratch.

Poisoned. Not good, but not as bad as it could be given Amazons went through a training period to build a resistance to many toxins.

But a resistance didn't mean she didn't feel sluggish, and she couldn't fight against the next tentacle that gripped her and plucked her from the water, waving her in front of the kraken. The bastard practically grinned, at least she assumed the wide-open mouth and fetid gurgling spelled excitement.

"No one's chewing on my tough carcass today," she muttered. She lifted her arm, intending to throw the sphere bomb into the kraken's gaping mouth.

The missile rolled from fingers gone lifeless.

Oops.

She peeked down at the waves that swallowed it. And counted. Odd how her awareness remained acute. It was her body that refused to move. Paralysis sucked.

As would death by ingestion.

Water bubbled below them. The bomb had exploded and not done a mote of damage to the sea monster.

Gross monster breath rolled over her as the tentacle brought her closer to the kraken's mouth.

"Unhand her, beast!" Dex yelled. A sphere went flying past her, falling short of the mouth.

If a kraken could gloat, this one did, its one giant eye smirking.

At least its eye taunted until it exploded with a gush. Ew. The poker Dex had flung hung from the remains, but didn't kill the beast.

The appendage resumed its course to the mouth.

I am about to become a Kraken's breakfast.

"Oh no you don't," hollered her geek, who just wouldn't give up.

It seemed she wasn't the only one interested in seeing what he planned. The tentacle holding her turned, and that meant she could see Dex run from the far end of the cabin's rooftop before leaping.

For a moment, his legs ran on air, and he actually gained more distance. Back came his arm, the sinews in it bunching. His arm whipped forward, and the grenade left his hand. The glass sphere with its swirling colors soared, and the tentacle holding her turned to watch its flight.

The bomb disappeared into the black cavern of the kraken's mouth but didn't immediately explode. Damned delayed timer.

Dangling in the air, she wondered if Adexios had made it back to the safety of the cabin. A moment later she had her answer as a tentacle rose alongside her, holding him.

He shot her a smile. "Hi."

Hi? If she weren't paralyzed, she might have giggled. As it was, she did manage to expel a breath of air as the bomb finally exploded. She didn't feel the tentacle around her loosen, but she did notice she was falling. Her eyes remained open as she hit the water and then bobbed back up.

The sea tossed her, the agitation of the kraken's death churning the water. Waves washed over her face.

So this is how I die. Drowning. That sucked. Now how would her sisters dress her in her finest warrior garb and send her to the ever after by burning her body to ash, freeing her spirit to choose another host? A girl child born of an Amazon.

Except Valaska didn't die. Not yet. Oddly enough, her limp body floated on the waves, but for how long?

How long before she sank?

How long before another kraken or other sea monster came along and thought she was an easy snack?

Not long apparently.

A single eye on a long purple stalk rose from the water and blinked at her. Dex's sea monster pet had returned to finish the job.

She didn't even have the ability to call it a name when it sent a tentacle to grab her around the waist.

But she did think it. *Fucker.*

Chapter Twelve

*"If at first you don't succeed, cheat." From
Lucifer's Guide to Ultimate Domination*

The *S.S. Sushimaker* sliced through the waves of
the new sea that covered the wilds. Everywhere Lucifer
looked, he saw water, water, and more water.

And water wasn't really his element.

Lucifer glared as smoke seeped from his ears. He
turned his gaze toward the most likely culprit, and an
easy scapegoat. "If I find out you had something to do
with this, Neptune…" He let his threat trail into
ominous silence.

"Not me. But I do have to wonder who has this
type of power," Neptune added with a pensive mien as
he stroked his long, luscious beard, currently braided
with seashells. The guy grew great facial hair. It totally
woke the green monster within Lucifer named Envy,
which totally perked him up. Nothing like a little
coveting sin to brighten a miserable day. Jealousy also
gave him great ideas on how to shave the sea god's pride
off his chin.

Later. Right now, he had a situation to deal with.

"Where is this water coming from?"

"Not from the Styx or Darkling Sea," Charon
replied from where he stood at the helm, his admiral cap
perched atop his cowl. "The water levels on both have
risen. The low-lying villages on the edges have flooded.
If the water continues to rise, we will have to evacuate

more of the towns along the river."

"And put them where? We already have a housing shortage. These refuges have made it worse. The complaints department has now begun complaining to me that there's too much work. Totally unacceptable. It's cutting into my fornicating time. Maybe we should just toss those displaced souls into the abyss for recycling."

For the uninformed, the abyss was a bottomless pit at the center of the rings. It was a soul recycler of sorts. Once a damned one did their time, they could chose to end their current existence and start anew, in a fresh body back on the mortal plane.

Reincarnation. Sounded great, right? Kind of.

If a soul chose to fling themselves in the abyss, everything they knew, all of what they were, would vanish. Wiped clean.

Oddly enough, many souls preferred to eke out an existence in Hell rather than take that final step.

It drove Lucifer crazy. Who wanted to stay in the pit? He only stayed here because of his job description. Lord of Sins, King of Hell, Eater of Souls. Not that he actually dined on them, unless he was really in the mood for shits and giggles.

Newbies always screamed loudest, not having realized they couldn't actually die. Eventually any part eaten grew back. What sucked was apparently the souls eventually got used to the pain. A flaw he was working on.

Just like Lucifer would have to lean on the committee responsible for making Hell the worst plane to live on to step up its game. He couldn't have people enjoying themselves living here. It would ruin his reputation.

"You can't just toss souls into the recycling pit," Charon said.

"Why not? It's cruel. It's unjust. It's totally me," Lucifer exclaimed.

"It's also highly efficient," the old ferry master pointed out.

The devil made a face. "Ugh. I will not have it said that I'm efficient."

Neptune cleared his throat. "Um, instead of worrying about moving the souls, perhaps, instead, we should find the cause for the flooding and take care of it."

"Much as I hate to agree with surfer dude, Neptune is right. We need to teach a lesson to the person or thing that thought it could brazenly come into your world and take a chunk for themselves." Charon's statement struck the right chord with Lucifer.

"Yes, we do need to school the interloper. Crush the miscreant like a bug. Then bring them back to life so we can crush them again," Lucifer agreed, smashing his fist into his palm.

"You both seem to forget that we have yet to figure out who is behind this travesty," Neptune pointed out.

"I see a certain bearded merdude is peeved someone's got a bigger ocean than him," Charon snickered.

"Am not."

"Oh ho. Someone's jealous he's got a smaller sea." Lucifer waggled his brows and grinned.

A scowl on Neptune's face only brought more attention to that damnable beard. "It's not size that matters," was his huffy reply.

"The whole-size-doesn't-matter thing is what men with little dicks keep saying to try and convince the women it's true," Lucifer said under his breath.

Charon snickered.

Neptune glared. "Just because not all of us choose to flaunt our junk doesn't mean I'm not hung like a whale."

A fresh breeze with a hint of tropical flowers caressed Lucifer's skin. They had company.

"Woman on deck. Hide the blow-up dolls and porn magazines," he shouted. Let it not be said that he wasn't a gentleman.

With a girly mince of steps and a swirl of skirts, Gaia joined them. "Hello, boys. I see I'm not interrupting much."

"On the contrary, we were discussing important matters, wench."

"You were talking about your penises. Why am I not surprised?" Gaia said with a roll of her eyes.

"Argh, woman. Do not use that word.

"Penis."

Lucifer cringed, and he wasn't alone. Even Charon's cowl shriveled around the edges.

Mother Nature's laughter tinkled, silvery bells in a gentle breeze. It set his teeth on edge with its cuteness. To combat it, he scratched his hefty package.

Since she was always checking him out, on account of his awesomeness—and admit it, his superiority was very attractive—she noted his manly gesture.

A gasp escaped her full, perfect-for-sucking lips as she took in his impressive outfit. Handpicked by the devil himself.

"Are you wearing a sailor suit?" she asked.

"With a few modifications," he added with a large helping of pride. He angled his hips forward. "I wasn't crazy about all that white, so I got the pants and shirt in a lovely black. The ascot, as you can see, has been hand-stitched with sharks."

"With horns," Neptune added, his voice choked. Probably in envy. Not everyone was blessed by Lucifer's ingrained sense of style.

"I also had them embroider the savage fish on my hat." Lucifer tapped the brim.

"Is it me or do I hear the theme song from *Jaws*?" she asked.

"It's all about the attention to detail," Lucifer confided.

Appearing faint, probably with lust because he rocked the whole suit, Gaia said, "Let's move on to other details."

"But I haven't even shown you the best part. I got a matching set of briefs also embroidered with—"

Gaia placed a finger against his lips. "Show me later, my horny devil. Right now, we should work on the flood situation."

He nipped and then sucked on the finger pressed against his mouth. "Yes, let us pull the plug on this problem so I can get to showing my underwear to my wench."

"Okay, gentlemen—"

Lucifer hacked.

"And rakish cads, what do we know?" she asked.

Lucifer summarized their knowledge so far. "We know nothing. Except the water is wet. And gross."

Closing her eyes, Gaia took a deep breath through her nose. A smile curved her lips as she remarked, "I don't know. I find the sea air kind of refreshing. Maybe it wouldn't be so bad. Let Hell flood, then we could do like those Italians did and have canals patrolled by gondolas."

"And seed the waterways with mutant crocodiles, sea serpents, and giant piranhas." Lucifer rubbed his chin as he envisioned the possibilities.

"You'd have to say goodbye to golf. As well as females suntanning on beaches," Neptune interjected.

"What? No more beach bunnies getting sand in their unmentionably delicious places?"

Gaia glared his way.

"Not that I would know or care about the taste, given you're the only pie I want to eat." Lucifer smiled. She didn't thaw. "Want me to prove it? There's a bed in the cabin."

"Focus," Charon reminded. "We are here looking for my useless son. You know, the one that's missing on account you sent him on a dangerous mission."

"An important one," Lucifer replied.

"You can come over and explain the importance of it to his mother anytime."

Lucifer couldn't hide a shiver. "Uh, no need to do that. We'll just find him."

"We'd better. We don't want a repeat of kindergarten when his mother lost it on that teacher."

What a wonderful nightmare that was. No one insulted Charon's son by calling him a brilliant student and future shining star. That teacher served as an example to all of Adexios' future educators.

"Incoming!" Charon said with a shout. Okay, not a real shout, but given it was at least a decibel louder than usual, Lucifer knew something cool was happening.

"Where's the danger? What is it? Someone fetch me my mace."

A blue imp, its fingers webbed and its eyes big and black, immediately slapped a can in his hand.

Lucifer regarded the nozzled canister and sighed. He hated training new demonic cabin boys. "Not that kind of mace. The big and heavy kind with the spikes on the end."

While he waited for his weapon of choice, Charon explained the nature of the threat.

"Radar shows a torpedo off the starboard side."

"A bomb? Are you sure it's not a giant black shark? Maybe a mutant mermaid?" the devil asked, unable to hide his hope.

"How many times do I have to tell you that mutant mermaids don't exist," Gaia muttered.

"Then where did that story I heard in that tavern down by the waterfront about the three-breasted vixen who rose from the sea come from? Explain that."

She sighed. He heard that sound often as she bowed before the greatness that was him and his impeccable logic.

Envy him, for he was perfect.

And now, high five for indulging in the vice of envy.

"Impact in five seconds."

"Meaning big hole in the boat, followed by an epic sink. Hope you brought swimsuits. Given I am a gifted swimmer, I can carry someone to safety if need be," Neptune said with a sly look at Gaia, followed by boasting flex of his arm pipes.

As if Lucifer's woman noticed. She only had eyes for one horny devil.

But just in case, it never hurt to save the day—and earn her gratitude. "I am not in the mood to get my hair wet." Not when it took an hour daily to straighten and threaten his curly locks into compliance.

Lucifer stared into the water and visually located the incoming missile. *Gotcha.* He snapped his fingers. The torpedo disappeared from sight, and in the distance, a geyser of water shot into the air. "Oh yeah. Who's the star, baby!" He fist pumped, and Gaia clapped.

"You're the star, but next time, could you add a

little more pizazz?" she asked. "I expect flashier from you."

Charon grumbled. "Fuck flashy. Get those fingers snapping or brace yourself because we have four more inbound. Different directions. Impact in less than forty-five seconds."

"My wench wants a little more flash?" Lucifer tugged on his ascot and tipped his sailor hat rakishly. He held out his hand to Gaia. "Shall we dance?"

"I would love to." She took his fingers with a smile, managing, even after all this time, to send a jolt of electrical awareness into him.

How splendid she was. And light on her feet.

He spun her away from him, his hand gripping hers so that she snapped at the end of the spin. She smiled coyly then looked away.

She clicked her fingers in the air.

A waterspout erupted on the side of the ship, bursting high into the air and showering the deck in fragrant water lilies.

Show off. Just another sinful thing about her to admire.

He tugged her back into him, his hand anchoring itself at her waist as they did a four step, followed by a little skip, and then an intense body-to-body hug as they stared into each other's eyes.

Fire licked between them. He clicked his fingers.

The missile exploded in the air with a whistle and a bang.

Gaia laughed. "It's always fireworks with you."

"And volcanoes exploding," he replied with a leer before doing a rapid cha-cha-cha to the stern.

He dipped his woman, and she arched back, her breasts threatening to spill from her gown.

Don't threaten. Spill! Spill!

Alas, Gaia had a firm grip on gravity, and her luscious boobs remained hidden. But she was his woman for a reason.

She snapped her fingers, and a geyser of water shot into the air, the delicate sprinkle of its drops strategically landing in on her upper half, soaking the fabric and delineating her very fat nipples.

Only centuries of dance kept him from stumbling as he whirled her around in a spinning-fast samba to the aft. He drew her to his chest, staring into her eyes, aware of the danger yet unable to resist the foreplay.

He let the torpedo grow closer and closer.

"What are you waiting for?" she panted against his lips.

This. He pressed his mouth against hers just as the rumble hit underneath the ship, lifting it and giving it a shake. The severity of the shock forced him to keep Gaia close and spin a cocoon of power around them.

"Are you protecting me?" she said, breathless and not because of their dance.

"Never."

"Never?"

He relented a little. "I would never shame myself by acting heroic and saving you. However, I can assure you that, if some brazen fool were to harm you, I would avenge you."

"Good to know," a strange voice announced from starboard.

Whirling around, Lucifer made note of the guy who'd managed to sneak up on them.

The man with the olive skin, thick dark beard—another guy with a beard, which made Lucifer wonder if it was time to either grow his own or ban them—regarded him with a haughty stare while wearing the most boring outfit.

A navy blue cable-knit sweater with jeans and deck shoes. Not a single ducky or shark, nothing. Some people had no style.

"Who are you? And where did you get that stupendous submarine?" The sleek and superbly long underwater craft bobbed in the waves alongside the *S.S. Sushimaker*. While the captain himself might bore someone to tears with his mundane style, his submarine was the opposite.

Painted a vivid purple, it sported a fierce eyeball on the side, actual metal jagged teeth on the front, and a periscope.

I always wanted a periscope.

"I built it myself," the ill-dressed guy replied.

"Really? Wow, that makes the fact I'm just going to take it from you even more awesome." Because a stolen submarine was even better than a custom one.

"Take?" The laughter boomed across the water and echoed. Cool trick. "I'd like to see you try."

"Like? Oh, you won't like it. Fear, yes. Possibly blubber and wet your pants, too. Nobody ever enjoys my takeovers. Something about unnecessary roughness." Lucifer rolled his eyes. "Pussies."

"Do you know who I am?"

"No. And your name doesn't matter. Unless you owe me something. Then I'll want it so that my accountant doesn't give me heck for not giving him the proper paperwork. Such a stickler for details those types."

"I am Captain Nemo."

Lucifer blinked.

"Also known as Prince Drakkar."

Lucifer yawned.

"Am I boring you?"

"Totally. And here I thought you were going to offer a challenge. But you're just another one of those villains who likes to yap, yap, yap, instead of act."

"Try more like a mastermind who's spent the last minute or so distracting you and your crew while my missile gets into position."

BOOM!

The impact was felt in every plank, rivet, and atom of the ship.

"We've been hit!" Charon said two octaves higher than usual.

Which was worrisome, but not as worrisome as the fact that the impact sent Mother Nature, who was leaning against the rail studying this Nemo fellow, flying.

She soared in the air, green skirts fluttering, and she landed right in the arms of the other captain.

"Oh my," she gasped. "I seem to be your prisoner. Whatever shall I do?"

Lucifer could have snickered at her feigned routine. Gaia was more than capable of taking down this upstart.

Except the upstart pulled something from his pocket, a giant needle, that he plunged into her arm. Gaia didn't even manage to shoot more than a single flower from her fingertips before wilting in Nemo's grasp.

The bastard had drugged her!

Totally unacceptable. "Unhand my fiancée," he demanded. Not liking at all the fact this other fellow was putting his hands on his girl.

"You want her, then come and get her, if you dare." With an evil chuckle that he must have gotten high grades on in villain university, the Nemo guy jumped into an open hatch, with Gaia still in his arms.

The hatch sealed shut as the sub began to sink.

"Do something," Lucifer yelled at Charon when his finger snaps refused to affect the sub. Some kind of anti-magical barrier deflected all his attempts.

"I'm trying to get our bulkheads sealed so we don't sink," snapped his usually calm boat master.

The devil turned to Neptune. "Well, don't just stand there. Jump in the water and do something sea god-ish."

Neptune turned wide eyes his way. "Dude. That was Captain Nemo."

"Never heard him."

"How can you have never heard of him? He's famous."

But in need of a better publicist since the name didn't ring any bells. "I've never seen him around before."

"Probably because he's not supposed to exist. Captain Nemo is a fictional character in a book."

"Tell that to the guy who just brazenly stole my woman. If I didn't hate him so much, I'd admire him for his balls." Because only someone with a massive set would intentionally screw with the devil.

Kidnap my woman, will he? Lucifer had many tortures for someone like that.

The waves closed over the purple submarine, severing his visual link to Gaia. The spot she'd taken over in his heart—and guarded with a vicious, possessive jealousy—felt empty. This Nemo character, and his damned machine, had cut the essence of her spirit from him.

Lucifer didn't like it one bit. "Follow them," he demanded as the sub sank from sight.

"This ship is meant to float on the waves, not under them," Charon reminded.

"Excuses!" Usually he'd applaud the diverting of

blame. However, this affected him directly. A scowl pulled Lucifer's brows together. "I blame you for this, Charon! I told you we needed a submarine."

"But you don't like confined spaces," his admiral reminded.

True. As a man of grandeur, only large spaces would do. "If we don't have a submarine in our fleet, then how am I supposed to save Gaia?"

"You intend to play hero?" Neptune practically fell over in shock.

"An unfortunate turn of events." Lucifer grimaced. "Sometimes a devil's gotta do ugly things to reap the reward."

"The reward being killing that nervy bastard, Nemo."

"No, the reward will be debauching a grateful fiancée of mine when I save her sweet buttocks from the guy who will be feeding the troll guests at our engagement feast."

Chapter Thirteen

"After a hard day's work, be sure to celebrate your unlife. Half off all grog and whiskey at Barnacle Jim's if you buy the Cajun-dusted petrified clams." This message is sponsored by the Bartenders Association of Hell.

When Adexios regained consciousness, it was to find himself lying face first on sand. At least that was how it felt to his face. Gritty, kind of warm, with that certain smell only beaches had.

Opening his eyes, he could further add that it was indeed sand, the obsidian kind that gleamed in the sunlight.

It was a struggle, man against body, to turn his face to the side. Mission accomplished, he even managed an "Oof" of surprise.

Lying only a few feet from him was Valaska, staring right back.

Adexios would have loved to say something clever like, *How you doing?* However, it wasn't just his general geekiness that stopped him but the fact the paralyzing agent had yet to leave his body. His tongue refused to move from the bottom of his mouth.

So he tried to talk with his eyes.

Are you okay?

She rolled her eyes. *Duh. I'm alive.*

He blinked a few times. *Any idea of where we are?*

She stared. *Does it matter?*

His ass was getting uncomfortably warm in the warm rays from the sun.

Sun?

Hell didn't have a sun. At least not a real one. With a great deal of effort, he flopped to his back and stared overhead.

Blue sky. Wispy clouds. Bright, blazing sun. White seagull swooping in low.

Splat.

The hot liquid ran down his chest, and he managed a garbled, "Gonna roast you over a fire."

A husky chuckle met his words as Valaska managed to reply in a rusty voice. "Sounds delicious."

As the effects of the poison wore off, mobility returned. Adexios managed to sit up then struggle to his knees. Valaska recovered even more quickly, bouncing to her feet and putting her body through some exercises.

She lifted her arms high above her head, her naked breasts popping forward with delicious intensity.

Down she bent to touch her toes, and he leaned back on his haunches to see her tight ass projecting upwards.

Straightening, she caught him watching and smiled. A smile full of naughty wickedness.

Lifting her leg, she grasped it and raised it high, very high, very exposing.

Since she stood fairly close, he had a great view. He didn't avert his gaze from the pink splendor of her sex, nor did he hide the evidence of the effect she had on him.

"I see your body parts are working again, as normal," she said with a laugh before setting down the one leg and grabbing the other for a stretch.

"Is anyone from Hell ever truly normal?" he replied, his usual answer coined the first time he'd disappointed a girl in the bedroom with the fact that he didn't sport mutant parts.

"Normality is a rarity in many cases. But speaking of normal, is it me, or is this place on the mortal side?"

Casting a peek around, Adexios squinted as he took better stock of their location before answering.

The black sandy beach extended into the distance before blurring out of sight. Bright blue waves lapped at the glistening dark sand while, at their back, a lush green jungle loomed, but not too deep because towering over it all was a mountain. So far, these things could technically appear in Hell. Most telling of all was the true sun in the sky emitting a bright glare. His quick strip to rush to Valaska's aid meant virgin-white flesh getting roasted.

The blazing heat also dried the seagull goop on his chest. Ick. Striding down to the waves, he knelt in the warm water and splashed himself clean.

Valaska followed him. "Any ideas on what we should do now?"

"You're asking me?" He paused in his bathing to peek at her. His eyes never made it past her shaven mound. Since she was asking for ideas, perhaps he should suggest fashioning some clothing from leaves or something so he wouldn't have to fight this urge to pounce on her and ravish her.

"My skills lie more in the realm of killing or tracking things. What to do when stranded on an isle in the mortal realm? Not covered in the Amazon guide."

"There's a guide?" Then again, why was he so surprised? The Ferrymen had one, too. It also didn't cover this scenario.

"We are not just a bunch of savage women who run amok killing things." She smiled. "We are a bunch of savage women who run around with purpose killing things."

The jest drew a chuckle from him. "Duly noted. As to what we should do? Good question. I wish I could bloody well see." Or at least protect his exposed manparts from the deadly rays of the sun. "I don't suppose it's too much to hope my glasses or knapsack washed up on shore?" While he could see the world in blurry color, sharp focus would be better.

Plop.

Something landed in the sand at his feet.

"My glasses!" he exclaimed. "Where did those come from?" He quickly jammed them on his nose, bringing the world into focus. He stood for a better view just as she shouted, "Duck!"

"Really? Ducks. I didn't think they did tropical islands because—Oomph." The knapsack hit him square in his recently cleaned chest. He staggered a bit but didn't drop his bag, mostly because he was so damned happy to see it. With the supplies he had stashed within it, at least now they stood a chance.

And all because of a certain sea monster.

A long purple stalk with a familiar eyeball bobbed on the waves a few yards out.

Adexios waved. "Thank you!"

"I think that's the monster that saved us after the kraken fight," Valaska said.

"I told you being nice would pay off."

"Pay off for you maybe." Valaska glanced around. "Where's my stuff?" She turned to glare at the eyeball, bobbing on the waves.

"I don't suppose you saved her things too?" Adexios asked, giving the sea monster his prettiest eyes.

"Oh, please. That's never going to w—"

Schwing. The sword came arcing out of the water and spun at her. Without batting an eye, Valaska timed its movement just right and crowed, "My precious," as soon as her hand curled around the pommel of the blade.

More wet articles followed. Valaska snatched each and every one out of the air, except for the thong. That Adexios reached out to grab.

He stuffed it in the pockets of the shorts he'd pulled from his bag and donned. At her arched brow in his direction, he grinned. "I'm keeping them for luck."

"We'll need luck to get off this island."

"How do we know it's an island?"

"Logical guess. But I would love to be proven wrong."

Alas, he feared she was right. It took them only a few hours to do a half-circuit of the island and note the smooth black sand ringing it, the clear blue waves lapping at it, and the sun, a merciless burner of skin, in the sky.

They made it only partway around because the large mountain in the middle extended in a ridge, high and sheer enough to block their passage.

"Maybe we'll have better luck on the other side?" she said as she gazed thoughtfully at the hump of black stone.

Adexios doubted it, which was why he flopped to the ground with a groan. "And I thought Hell was hot."

"You do seem to be rather sensitive to natural daylight," was her diplomatic reply.

"If this is your way of saying I look like I'm related to a fire demon, then thanks."

"Stop complaining. We need to come up with a plan."

"You mean like resting on this nice beach and hoping a boat comes along to rescue us?" A boat with air conditioning and those icy drinks with little umbrellas in them.

"Optimism is one of the things our boss hates," she noted.

"Not if it's false hope."

She snorted. "Smart ass."

"I know."

"Given the beach route is a wash, maybe we should explore inland. At least then you'll get some shade, and maybe we'll find some food and water."

Water might be nice, given the canteen he'd pulled from his pack was now dry.

Time for a refill. "I've got food, and I can get more…" His voice trailed off as consternation stole his words. He jammed his hand into the pocket holding the interdimensional rip to his mom's fridge, only his fingers met canvas, not the cold glass shelf with Tupperware containers and plastic water bottles. "My fridge! It's gone."

"I wonder if the magic stopped working once we crossed into the mortal realm."

Stupid mundane world with its rules on science. "What a total rip-off. I am going to talk to the complaints department when I get back."

"There you go with that optimism again." She grinned. "But in this case, I like it. Can I come along when you ream them out?"

Had she just suggested they continue their association past this mission? The idea pleased him an inordinate amount. Not that he said how happy it made him. His reply was a more manly, "Yeah, sure, if you want."

What he wanted, too, was to find a nice shady spot, strip those clothes from her, and finish what they'd started. Funny how his attraction for her only intensified, even if she was covered in a sheen of perspiration and her hair frizzed from the tight braid she'd weaved. There was more to like about Valaska than just her exterior. He was finding himself rather liking her attitude as well. She was pretty damned awesome, and he'd have loved to show her just how much he liked her.

Unfortunately, she seemed intent on hacking at the foliage with her sword, lamenting the lack of dangerous wildlife, and totally staying dressed, no matter how much he tried to get her clothes to fall off with the power of thought.

Wait a second. Maybe he did have the power of mental suggestion because, one minute, she was cutting them a swathe through the jungle, and the next she was stripping!

Holy shit. It worked. He was a mental force to be reckoned with.

Or she'd found a refreshing-looking pool of water.

In the midst of the wild greenery, a veritable oasis appeared, about thirty feet across and lined with dark sand. The water gleamed with crystal clarity, clear enough that they could see a colorful school of fish darting in the shallows.

Without hesitation, Valaska immersed her naked body into the liquid and let out a sinful sigh. She floated on her back, the tips of her breasts bobbing.

"Are you coming?"

Give me another minute and I might. Except she didn't mean the orgasmic come. Didn't matter. He wanted some of what she was enjoying.

It didn't take him long to shed his sweaty clothes, drop his glasses on the pile, and dive in after her.

The cool water took some of the sting from his skin and refreshed him. He surfaced and joined her in floating on his back.

"This feels so fucking good," he said, his eyes closed, basking in the relaxing moment.

At least he meant to. Someone with slick skin sank him when she pounced and wrapped strong limbs around him.

He surfaced in her grip to find their faces only inches apart.

Valaska's eyes shone with mirth. "Hello, Dex."

"Hi," was his cautious reply.

"So it occurs to me that we almost died in battle."

"But didn't."

"Almost drowned, too."

"But survived."

"You're right. We prevailed, which means we need to celebrate."

"I'm pretty sure I don't have any cake."

She laughed. "We don't need bakery treats to celebrate. I've got a much better idea in mind."

A good thing he could touch bottom, as she locked her ankles around his waist and her arms around his neck. Then she kissed him.

She's kissing me!

And not just embracing him with her lips, but her tongue, too. Whatever initial surprise he might have felt at her brazen sensual assault disappeared quickly at the touch of her tongue, teasing the seam of his lips.

He let her in, let her take control of the kiss. But only for now.

Adexios had things he wanted to do to this woman. Dirty things. And, in this, he would have his way.

His hands cupped the fullness of her ass, squeezing the firm cheeks. His erect cock was trapped between their bodies, the hot core of her sex pressing it and teasing it with what would come.

While he loved having her wrapped all around him, it wasn't conducive for exploration. And he so wanted to explore.

The beauty of a jungle basin of water was the sandy shore and soft, fragrant plants lining it—none of them sporting teeth or thorns.

He carried her to the spot shaded by a large overhanging tree.

She laughed as he laid her gently down upon the warm sand. "Always so controlled, Dex."

"Not really," he replied before taking her mouth in a fierce kiss.

With Valaska, there was no holding back the passion. No calm or measured acts. He devoured her mouth, nipping her lips and sucking on her tongue.

But that wasn't enough. Who cared if he'd explored parts of her body already? He needed to reacquaint himself by tasting it. Those nipples, surely they weren't as wonderful as he recalled.

His lips latched around a protruding bud, and she gasped. Oh my, they proved even more splendid than he remembered. He spent a few minutes teasing those responsive buds, torturing them with his mouth and teeth until they stood tight and erect.

She moaned a protest when his lips left them to move downward, over the ridge of her belly down to the bared splendor of her mound. He kissed the skin there, a surge of pleasure making him growl when she shuddered.

This close to her sex, the aroma of her arousal was unmistakable. Fragrant.

Delicious…

He didn't just want a taste. He *needed* it.

Her legs spread wide, and he dove on her

offering, lashing his tongue against the velvety folds of her sex, tasting the sweetness.

And then the sweetness was taken from him!

"Bring it back!" he complained.

"I intend to," she replied. "Once you get on your back."

To emphasize her wish, she flipped him then straddled him, in reverse. It didn't take a genius to know what she intended.

As her lips found the head of his swollen cock, she lowered her sex to his face.

Was there anything more spectacular than a woman who believed in a 69? The only problem was her obvious enjoyment of his shaft made it hard to concentrate.

Lick her sweet clit. Swirl his tongue around it.

Gasp as she bobbed her head low on his cock. Groan as she suctioned it hard.

Stab his tongue within her silken folds, taste her cream, feel her muscles squeezing, look for something to hug.

Arch the hips as she nipped the tip of him then dig his fingers into her ass checks and worry her clit between his lips as she licked him with slow decadence.

A few times he thought he'd come, and she knew it, too. She'd stop and simply blow on his wet skin. He did the same to her. When her body grew too tense, he stopped, watched her quivering, and then said fuck it and dove back on.

He wanted to make her come. More than once if he could. So when he felt her tension coiling, he didn't stop, even as she lost her rhythm on his cock.

He didn't relent, even as she whimpered and her body tensed.

He continued to lap as she cried out his name,

"Dex," in one long, drawn-out syllable.

The waves of her pleasure vibrated on his tongue, which stabbed within her channel. But he didn't enjoy it for long.

Valaska wasn't one to let the man take the lead, not when she wanted more. She pulled her still-pulsing sex from his lips and, in one smooth motion, impaled herself on his cock.

He yelled. He also bucked, but she was firmly seated in a reverse cowgirl.

His hands found her waist, not that she needed help or guidance. She bounced perfectly fine on his throbbing dick all on her own, each thrust in and out drawing his sac tighter and tighter.

"Fuck. Fuck. Fuck." He couldn't help chanting as the pleasure grew more and more intense.

He wasn't going to be able to hold on much longer. She moved faster, slamming up and down on him, her buttocks cushioned by his groin, his cock sheathing so deep.

The pulse of her climax squeezed his shaft superbly tight. So tight. Oh fuck. He couldn't help himself.

He came, the heat of his seed shooting and her channel fisting him and drawing every ounce of pleasure it could wring.

It took forever to come down from the high, or so it felt as his heart beat rapidly and his eyes refused to open, even as she collapsed beside him.

But his arms still worked enough to draw her close to his side, close enough that he could place a kiss on her forehead and wistfully think, *I wish we could stay like this forever.*

Except, apparently, he said it, didn't think it, and while Valaska said, "This is nice," someone else joined the conversation with a gurgled, "Glerg. Blerg. Harg!"

Chapter Fourteen

"Don't waste what you kill. There's a recipe for everything." A quote from Cannibal Carol's best-selling cookbook.

Explosive sex was no excuse for not paying attention to her surroundings. In her defense, though, Valaska never expected an enemy to come from the crystal pond they'd swum in.

Water dripping from their slimy and mottled green skin, a pair of ugly beasts leered at Valaska and Adexios. Humanoid in shape, but amphibious in appearance, with bulbous eyes, flat noses with only two holes to mark it, and webbed hands. They kind of reminded her of frogs, but a tad more dangerous than the hopping, delicious-when-deep-fried kind.

The duo, baring pointed teeth, wore loincloths on their hips and held spears with wicked pointed tips.

Having sprung to her feet, with her sword in hand of course—as if she ever let it stray far from reach—she bent her knees into a half-crouch to face the pair.

Only two foes? She wouldn't even break a sweat—unlike the workout Dex had given her body. Her geeky lover sure knew how to play her body and leave her panting. She couldn't help but cast a glance his way and noted he was scrounging through his pack.

Does he have a spray to fight frogs in there, too? It wouldn't surprise her at this point.

The slight distraction as she pondered Dex's many surprising levels didn't mean she missed the spear jabbing at her. Since she wasn't really into bodily piercings, she leaned her body sideways, letting the pointed tip slide harmlessly past her.

Before the frogman could retract his lunge, with a twirl of her blade, she sliced through his pole.

The pointed tip hit the sand, and the creature made an angry sound. "Horgblar!"

"I think you pissed him off," Dex remarked from behind her.

"Good."

Her now spearless opponent's slimy companion lunged next, and his pointed weapon met the same fate to much gargling and burbling curses in frog-tongue.

The green duo tossed the remains of their spears to the ground and dropped into a half-crouch.

Awesome, they weren't done playing. She grinned. "Bring it, slimeballs."

Except they didn't make a move to tackle her, as expected.

She didn't need Dex's shouted, "Watch out for their tongues," to know she should not let the extremely long and forked pink appendages touch her skin.

"Bad froggies," she taunted. "Trying to give me tongue on our first date."

One tongue met the same fate as a spear while the second narrowly missed her.

"Miss me. Miss me. Now you gotta kiss me. Not!"

Practically busting a bulbous eye in rage, the frogman shot his tongue back at her, but before she could sever it, Dex was there, shaking a powder on it.

As the second frogman sucked back in its slimy appendage, it warbled and hopped, even more upset than his tongueless companion.

Valaska had to ask, "What did you do to it?"

"Cayenne pepper. I still had a shaker of it in my bag. I like my food spicy."

While she preferred her food dead. Then again, when a few quick slices left the frogmen on the ground, green heaps of rancid flesh, she decided that perhaps now was not the time to try that recipe Carol had told her about that suggested wrapping amphibious legs in leaves and roasting them over some hot coals.

Wiping her sword clean, she kept an eye on the water. *Surprise me once, shame on me. Surprise me twice and I'll have to go on a killing spree so word doesn't get back to my tribe.*

As Dex dressed, he felt a need to talk. "Do you think there's more of them around?"

"I hope so." While short-lived, the giant froggies had provided entertainment.

Then again, so did Dex. What an adept lover he proved to be. And an even better companion. Valaska was used to fighting battles on her own, constantly proving herself and fighting to stay alive in a cutthroat world where it was every woman for herself.

Yet Dex, while not a classic warrior, kept coming to her aid.

She knew her Amazon sisters would mock and shame her for allowing it, but…well…Valaska kind of thought it was cute. She'd never had someone come to her aid before. Especially not a man.

A man who had dressed, even though they needed to go for a swim.

"Should we head back to the beach?" he asked as he hefted his pack on his back.

"The beach has nothing for us. I say we find out where these creatures came from."

"There might be more of them."

She smiled. "We should be so lucky."

He might have sighed, but he did so with a smile. "Since I wouldn't want you to accuse me of being a gentleman, do you want to lead the way?"

Did she ever! She'd begun to wade into the water, sword in one hand, when Dex cleared his throat.

"Aren't you forgetting something?"

He held up her damp clothes.

"Does my nakedness bother you, Dex?"

"Very much. I can't think straight when you're flashing that much flesh."

She grinned. "Good. Stay close and try not to lose sight of me. I have a feeling we're going to have to go for a little swim."

"Don't worry," he muttered. "I can't seem to take my eyes off your ass."

Being a warrior didn't mean she didn't feel a spurt of warmth at his words.

She walked as far as she could into the pool of water. She could easily tell that the creatures hadn't come from the sandy beach edges, but there, at the far end of the pond, a heap of black stone rimmed it. Kicking toward that rock, once she reached it, she treaded water for a moment while she checked it out.

Nothing above the water line gave any clue. The rock façade extended fairly high, but she didn't see any crevices large enough for something to hide in.

Given frogs were aquatic creatures, a search underwater seemed in order.

A deep breath to fill her lungs and then she dove under the water for a closer peek. The black stone extended down, far down, deeper than expected. She followed the stony wall, sword in hand, just in case. And a good thing, too.

A green head poked from a dark shadow in the

stone, close to the bottom.

As it rotated to peer upward, a jab of her sword downward impaled the frogman before he spotted her. Instant death meant he didn't thrash. She used her sword to pull him out and let his body float away. She then kicked back to the surface.

"I found a tunnel."

"And company, I see," Dex remarked as the corpse floated to the surface several feet away.

"Ready to go find some more?"

"Does insanity run in my family?"

She blinked at him. "Doesn't it run in everyone's?"

He laughed. "Go. I'll follow."

How she enjoyed the fact that he didn't attempt to change her mind with stupid questions like, "How long is the tunnel?", "How will we breathe?", or "What if there's more enemies?"

Nope. Instead, he leaned close and brushed his lips against hers with a whispered, "Go get 'em!"

Sigh. If she wasn't careful, she might just fall in love with the guy.

Gasp.

Wouldn't that horrify her Amazon sisters? Funny, how she wasn't repulsed by the idea.

Taking a deep breath, she dove back down and headed right for the tunnel. She went in, sword point first, just in case there was someone in the way. There wasn't. A shame, then again, given the tunnel wasn't all that wide, it was probably a good thing.

Adrenaline coursed through her veins, her senses alive with anticipation. In the pitch-black, it wasn't exactly easy to see. The enemy could be right ahead of her, and she wouldn't see them.

But darkness wasn't the only thing she had to

contend with. The tunnel wasn't short. She kicked for what seemed like forever. Kicked so long her lungs burned and she wondered how Dex fared.

I hope he doesn't drown. It surprised her to realize she would be sad if he died. She rather liked having him around.

Just when she thought her lungs might burst, she noted a faint light ahead. Fluttering her feet even harder, she shot toward the illumination, the last of her breath emerging in bubbles that tickled her face. Air loomed straight ahead. She gave herself one last burst of speed and broke the surface of the water to find herself in a cave.

But not just any cave. A really big cave that held quite a few more of the frogmen. And they were waiting for her and Dex.

No sooner had his head appeared beside hers than tongues shot out from numerous directions. More than she could handle while treading water. Dammit!

Sproing. The tips of a few tongues hit her flesh, leaving the most unpleasant sensation.

Argh. I've been slimed.

The thing that vexed her most, though, as she sank in the water, succumbing to their poisoned saliva, was the fact that she'd been taken down by frogs. The shame of it.

Chapter Fifteen

"It is up to you what to wear under your ferryman official robe, but keep in mind, the Styx has strong breezes." Charon's unofficial advice to newbies.

Waking naked on a chilly surface, exposed to anyone looking, Adexios really wished for his robe. Probably for the first time ever. Having gotten used to the coverage, and privacy, afforded by it, he found his recent forays into nudity quite troubling.

Unless he was naked with Valaska. Then he quite enjoyed it. However, his companion—whom more and more he was thinking of as his lover, and dare he hope something more?—wasn't close by, or at least not close enough to be touching him or emitting that vibe he always felt when she was near.

Where is she?

Given he didn't know the situation, other than the fact that he was kind of chilly—again on account of the whole naked thing!—he didn't move a muscle. But he did crack an eye a slit.

What he saw didn't reassure.

Bars. Thick ones, too. The solid metal rods were spaced just wide enough to maybe slide his hand through. He rolled his head just slightly, as if moving in his sleep. This gave him a view of the top of his cage, made of the same metal. He froze as he listened, wondering if anyone had noted his motion.

He heard the lapping of water and the occasional

guttural gurgle of what he assumed were the frogmen who'd caught him.

At least the poison on their tongues wasn't fatal. Merely a narcotic to put them to sleep. Of interest also was the fact that they hadn't immediately killed them.

What do they want?

He doubted he could just ask, and even if he did, it was doubtful he'd understand them.

A lull in the garbled conversation by the creatures enabled him to hear a soft snore. He recognized that noise.

Valaska was here! And alive, but apparently still sleeping.

Either she'd received a bigger dose of the sleeping slime or he had a stronger immunity to it.

Knowing she was out cold meant he delayed letting anyone know he was awake. No point in confronting their captors until he had her help.

Some men might find themselves intimidated by a strong woman, but Adexios had grown up with one. He had total respect for a female who could stand her ground and protect herself.

Adexios' mom didn't need his dad to fight her battles. She could handle herself. But that didn't mean she didn't enjoy having a man in her life. It just meant his mom and dad had a relationship that worked on a different level than other couples.

I'd like to see if we could make it as a couple.

But first they needed to get out of this dilemma. He was counting on her to have a plan.

It didn't take a genius to predict that, when she woke, she'd be peeved. And possibly deranged, given the drug the frogs secreted not only had a sleeping agent but a slightly hallucinogenic one as well. At least that was his theory, given Adexios could have sworn that, when he turned his head back to the side, a blurry squint showed him another cage with someone shoved inside. Not just any someone either if he recognized the trademark green dress. Only some really good drugs could make him think Mother Nature was also a prisoner.

Impossible, of course. As if anything like the frogmen, or anyone for that matter, could ever trap Gaia.

"Adexios, is that you?" the figment of his imagination asked.

Don't reply. Only crazy people talked to imaginary prisoners.

However, even if she didn't exist, not replying seemed so rude. And yeah, he didn't care if Lucifer didn't like his obsession with manners. It was a bad habit of his.

"Yes, it's me," he slurred. Not completely cleared of the sleeping drug apparently. What a pity they'd stripped him of his bag—and clothes!—before shoving him in the cage. He could have used a caffeinated energy drink right about now.

"Your father is looking for you."

"He is?" Probably because his mum had threatened something vile if he didn't. Dad's parenting skills were in line with the survival of the fittest motto. For example, Charon had tossed Adexios into the Styx when he was a small child in order to force him to learn how to swim and evade sea monsters. "Move your skinny little butt. He's right on your tail" proved great incentive to kick his feet as fast as he could for the ladder.

Adexios only learned many years later that the beast was in cahoots with his dad and never planned to eat him at all. Such happy memories.

He blinked back to the present, as Gaia started talking again.

"Of course Charon is searching, as is Lucifer, and they've even got Neptune helping, too. I was also on that mission until I got caught," she said with a pout.

As his body worked to expel the drugs, his senses sharpened, as did his eyesight—especially once he realized the lump under his head was his glasses. Adexios squashed them on his nose.

No longer myopic, he peered at Gaia and found himself shocked by her appearance. The Mother Nature he knew was a vibrant woman in her forties. Full-figured, with shining hair, sparkling eyes, clear skin, always impeccably dressed and smelling of flowers.

The woman in the cage alongside him was anything but.

The brown hair hung in dull hanks around a face gray with pallor. Dark rings circled her eyes, and the green gown she wore was stained and wrinkled.

"What happened to you?" he asked, realizing that she was not a hallucination. Someone had actually managed to capture Gaia. *Lucifer won't be happy.*

"I told you, I was caught." And she sounded quite miffed about it.

"By who?" Who other than Lucifer or another powerful deity had the strength to capture Mother Nature herself?

"It was partially my fault. I wanted to impress the boys, so I accidentally threw myself at Nemo when he attacked our ship."

"Nemo? As in *the* Captain Nemo? I thought he was just a character in a book."

"We all did. Wrong," she said with a buzzer noise. "Apparently he exists, and he's got a powerful ally aiding him. He came prepared because he had some kind of needle filled with a drug capable of making me pass out." Her tone relayed her incredulity.

He understood the feeling. "A drug that worked on you? But that's impossible."

"That's what I would have said, too, until it happened. When I woke, I was here, in this cage." She cast a baleful glare at the bars surrounding her, yet she didn't touch them. She remained huddled in the center, knees hugged to her chest.

"Can't you get out?" If anyone had the magic to make shit happen, it was Gaia.

"I've tried. But whoever planned this did their homework. They managed to find my weakness."

"You have a weakness?" Other than Lucifer, who, with his arrogance and cheesy sexual innuendos, had managed to snag the most eligible bachelorette on all the known planes of existence.

"Yes, even I have a weakness. All deities do, even omnipotent ones like myself."

"What is it?" What could bind Gaia?

Her lip curled. "Humanity's pollution. The unnatural decay of manmade products, artificially created smog emitted by all those factories and vehicles, and, deadliest of all, radioactive waste. These bars"—she waved a hand at them—"are made of irradiated metal. Just touching them burns me." She held out her hands, and he winced at the red blisters scoring her palms.

"You can't use your magic to escape?"

"I am impotent. Unable to draw upon my well of green energy, unable to even heal myself." How morose she sounded. So defeated.

"Surely Lucifer will come save you?"

She arched a brow. "Lucifer? Really? Have you met the demon? Or heard his views on heroism?"

Adexios blushed. "Yeah. I've heard it. So I guess a rescue by him is out of the question. If you don't mind me backtracking to Captain Nemo, do you have any idea why he wants us as prisoners?"

Gaia shrugged. "Your guess is as good as mine. I haven't seen Nemo since I woke in this cage, and those frogmen aren't very talkative. How did you end up here? Last we heard, you were camping in the wilds, except the wilds got flooded, and no one could find you."

His turn to shrug. "We found ourselves afloat on the new sea. However, someone wasn't crazy about us being there and called some krakens. During the course of the battle, we got paralyzed, and the next thing we knew, we found ourselves on the shore of an island on the mortal side."

"So we are on the Earth plane. I wondered about that. These creatures holding us prisoner are unlike anything I've ever encountered either on Earth or in Hell."

"If you've never seen them before either, where did they come from?"

"If I were to hazard a guess, wherever this Nemo fellow sprang out of. In other words, another plane."

Adexios' mind churned and slid puzzle-like facts together, looking for answers. "Do you think this has to do with whatever came out of that rip a little while back?"

"Probably. There is no such thing as coincidence. Although whoever is moving against us has yet to show their face or announce their intentions."

"Speaking of intentions, I don't know about you, but I'm really not keen on sticking around in this cage and seeing what they have planned."

"You have a plan for escape?" Gaia asked, her eyes lighting with a bit of the green spirit she was known for.

"I do now."

While he and Gaia spoke, his guise of sleep

forgotten, he'd taken stock of their surroundings. The cages holding them prisoner hung from the rocky ceiling of the cavern, over top a watery channel.

While the cave itself proved fairly large, at least two or three dozen feet tall and even longer in length, most of the floor was submerged in water. What wasn't submerged was a strip of sand where the frogmen converged, talking amongst themselves, ignoring their prisoners.

Adexios already knew there was a passage from the jungle pond to the cave, but given he could spot daylight at the far end of the cave, and the briny scent, it didn't take a brilliant mind like his to deduce there was a passage leading in from the sea.

Or should he say a front door for a curious sea monster with a crush on a certain ferryman?

A familiar eyeball on a purple stalk rose from the water, unseen by the frogmen huddled on the far shore.

Pressing his face against the bars he held, Adexios whispered, "Hey there, gorgeous."

"Wh-a-a-a?" slurred Valaska.

The fact that she replied startled him. He peeked over at Valaska and saw her peering at him with one bleary eye.

"About time you woke up," he teased. "You were about to miss the action as I save your naked ass."

"Saaaave?" She struggled to her knees, only to stop as both her eyes popped open to glare at her cage. "Are those bars?"

"We were captured by the frogmen."

Valaska collapsed on the floor of her prison. "Ugh. The shame. The horror."

While his Amazon lover lamented their fate, while also elucidating the various ways she planned to cook their captors, Adexios concentrated on a certain creature that hovered nearby.

"Hey, pretty eye," he whispered. "You found me. Such a smart sea monster."

The orb bobbed and blinked in obvious pleasure.

"I'll bet you'd like more chocolate."

Big waggle of the stalk.

"What a shame those nasty froggies took my knapsack with its stash," Adexios said with a deep sigh. "Why they're probably eating the last of that yummy chocolate now."

The eyeball pivoted to glare at the frogmen, who burbled and gurgled, oblivious to everything going on.

"If only I could get my backpack from them, I'd be so grateful."

Plop. The giant orb slipped under the water.

"Do you think it will work?" Gaia asked.

Judging by the screams as tentacles whipped from the water and dragged the frogmen to a watery, possibly crunchy, death, "I'd say we're better off than we were a minute ago."

In no time at all, the cave was quiet. Even Valaska stopped bitching long enough to peek through her bars and mutter, "I hate to say it, but that sea monster is really starting to grow on me."

"I wonder how she'd like moving into the Styx. I always wanted a pet," Adexios muttered as he stroked the moist skin of the eyeball's stalk. "Given what a good companion you're turning out to be, we should think of giving you a name, too."

"I vote for Tentacles-Off-My-Man." Valaska was back to glaring.

My man? Adexios hoped they mistook his shiver for one of cold and not pleasure.

"Her name is She-Who-Eats-Exquisitely-Tasty-Screamers," Gaia supplied. At Adexios' look, she shrugged. "Before I began dating Lucifer, I might have spent a few decades seeing a certain sea god. I got to know a few different aquatic languages."

"Hello, Sweets," Adexios said, having shortened her name to the first letter. "You don't mind if I call you that, do you?"

An eyelid batted, and Valaska groaned. "Give me a fucking break. Stop flirting with the thing and tell it to get your bag, would you? I hate cages."

"She has a point, Adexios. We should hurry before Nemo discovers his troops have been squished and he does something more drastic."

"Sweets, can you bring me my bag now? You'll get a treat," Adexios sang in his most beguiling voice.

Valaska made a noise. "If you ever use that tone with me, I'll smother you."

"Seeing as how I recall the last time you did proved quite enjoyable, you do realize that's not a deterrent?"

He caught the wicked smirk she aimed his way. "I know."

Shudder. "Hurry up, Sweets. I need to save my delicate lady."

"Did you just call me delicate?" The incredulity in her reply made him laugh.

"Yes. I'm hoping that will get me punished, too." How easy he was now finding it to say what he felt—and wanted to do.

His initial awe at Valaska still existed, but it was more an awe at how wonderful he found her and awe that she wanted him back. He no longer feared what she thought of him. Only an idiot wouldn't recognize they shared a mutual liking and attraction. Getting her to admit it out loud though…that might never happen, given her heritage. But Adexios could live with that, if he could live with her.

However, their relationship details would have to wait for later. Sweets had brought him his bag.

"Such a good girl," he crooned as he slid his fingers through the bar to clasp it.

While he couldn't fit the bag between the bars, he did manage to tie the straps to the solid rods while he rummaged in it looking for what he needed.

"Are you looking for a hacksaw to saw through the bars?" Valaska asked.

Gaia made a noise. "Of course not. Adexios is more a man of science and magic. He's probably got a potion to melt the things."

"Um, how about none of the above?" He placed his hellphone, located at the bottom of his pack, beside him and then dove back in for the chocolate bar he had stashed. He unpeeled it and, given Mother Nature was staring at him, shoved the wrapper in his bag instead of tossing it from the cage. He then flung the treat with a heartfelt, "Thank you!"

The chocolate was snatched mid-air, and the eyeball rolled in delight.

Valaska muttered, "Are you serious?" while Gaia giggled.

Ignoring them both, Adexios grabbed his phone and dialed, 6-6-6.

"Calling for help? From the devil no less. Might as well kill me now since I won't survive the shame." Valaska groaned.

"Don't you dare call Lucifer," Gaia hissed. "I'll never hear the end of it otherwise."

"Neither of you have to worry. Apparently I don't get signal in villainous, mortal-side caves." Adexios glared at the screen that flashed *No Signal, Dumbass.* "Why can't anything about this mission be simple?"

"Because it would ruin all the fun."

"Because simple is boring."

"Neither of you is helping," he replied as he dug around in his bag again. This time he pulled out a vial, and Gaia shouted, "Aha! I knew the boy had some acid hiding in there."

"*He* does, but only enough to pop one lock," Adexios replied as he glanced through the bars and judge the thickness of the lock holding the door shut.

"If you set me free, then I can use my sword to pop the others."

He glanced at Mother Nature to see if she objected.

Gaia shook her head. "Even if you freed me first, I don't know if I'd have the strength to do much. I'm going to need to touch soil, real soil, and plants to recharge my magical battery. And I don't see any of that in this cave. Free Valaska. She can then free us both."

With that plan in mind, Adexios stretched his arm through the bars while Valaska stretched as well. Their hands met, and for a moment, they both froze, staring at each other through the bars.

"You know, um, maybe after this is all over, we could get a drink or dinner or something?" he said.

Valaska snorted. "Is that your awkward way of asking me on a date?"

"Well, considering I've been told Amazons don't date, I'm not sure what to say, other than I want to keep seeing you."

"You will."

"While your flirting is adorable, time is ticking, children. Could we get on with this?"

The bottle left his hand as Valaska grasped it. It took only a few minutes for the corrosive agent to eat through the lock. Not that Valaska waited until it was done. Bracing her back against the bars, she kicked at the weakened door until it popped open. Then, she vaulted out, her half-tucked spin dive making her splice the water with barely a splash.

Moments later, she was on the shore and snagging her sword from the sand.

A new dilemma arose.

"I can't reach you," she remarked, eyeing his cage suspended high overhead.

"Loosen the chains holding us up." He pointed to the spot where the chains were hooked to the wall.

"Okay. But you might get wet."

Clang.

While her sword had no problem smashing the metal links, gravity worked all too well.

Adexios' cage went plummeting toward the water, only to stop short as a few tentacles grabbed it.

"Thank you, Sweets."

He ignored Valaska's grumble as his cage was deposited on the shore.

"My turn," Gaia sang.

"In a second. Let me just get Dex out of his first."

Valaska swung at the lock. On the second smashing strike, the door popped open, and Adexios stepped out.

Only to find himself crushed in a hug and his lips plastered in a kiss.

While no words were exchanged during this torrid embrace, Adexios managed to decipher a few things.

One, Valaska was very happy to see him. And, according to a certain body part of his, he was *really* happy to see her, too.

Second, he could have sworn the woman in his

arms was sending a mental vibe to someone or something behind them along the lines of 'Nananananana'.

He broke their embrace just long enough to ask, "Are you taunting my pet?"

"Just showing her who you belong to."

Oh.

"In that case, continue," he replied, diving back in to continue the embrace. Alas, a kiss was all they would have for the moment, as a certain spectator grew impatient.

"Excuse me, lovebirds, but do you mind disengaging your lips long enough to let me loose?"

"I guess it's true what they say," Valaska said as she pulled her mouth away. "The older you get, the crankier."

"Hey!" an affronted Gaia yelled. A second later a rumble shook the cavern.

"Uh-oh, I think you pissed her off," Adexios said.

"That wasn't me," Gaia informed them.

The cavern shook again, and the water began sloshing, which had them uttering simultaneously, "What the fuck!"

Sweets cast a worried look at him before sinking out of sight.

Not a good sign.

Another not-good sign was the fact that the water in the cavern appeared to be rising and getting rough.

"What's happening?" Valaska asked as she quickly grabbed the harness for her knife and strapped it to her ankle. Adexios made sure he secured his pack on his back and wished he had time to pull on pants. However, water already swirled around his knees, and kept rising.

"I don't know what's happening, but you should hurry and cut Gaia's cage loose."

"Forget that plan," Mother Nature shouted. "And might I suggest you get out of the water?"

The warning came too late, though.

The whirlpool that suddenly appeared suctioned the water that immersed them. Caught in the current, with nothing to grab onto but each other, he and Valaska found themselves drawn into the eye of the maelstrom.

"Hold on!" he yelled as they whipped around and around.

"Whee!" Valaska hollered back.

The spin tightened as they reached the bottom and the gaping dark hole then… Darkness.

Chapter Sixteen

"The best thing about making rules is breaking them." From Lucifer's memoirs, on sale now for $6.66 at all major online stores.

"Where is she? Where is my woman?" The devil's bellow was heard throughout the nine rings of the pit, and yet, despite everyone hearing his query, no one could give him an answer.

Gaia was gone, but not dead. *I would know if she was dead.* All of Earth would actually know if his woman had perished, seeing as how the world revolved around her.

But while knowing she lived provided some kind of relief, it didn't help him locate her. There wasn't so much as a whisper of her presence. And he'd looked. He'd put his entire legion to the task, ordering his minions to search all the nooks and crannies of Hell. He had his spies in Heaven looking just in case his brother was fucking with him again. Lucifer had his spirit spies in Limbo, a gray wasteland, sifting for signs of color, green in particular. The devil had pulled every string he had in the mortal plane seeking his wench.

Not a trace could be found, which meant he could do nothing.

Impotence wasn't something Lucifer handled well. Especially since this kind of impotence didn't have a pill to fix it. Even sending his horsemen out in the world to dispense a bit of rage didn't make him feel better.

"Where has he stashed her?" Lucifer paced his living room in front of the massive stone fireplace that blazed bright—it should, considering he kept it well fed with the bodies of the idiots who kept bringing him back empty reports.

His black Hessian boots gleamed as they struck the striated rock floor. The creases of his pants were sharp enough to slice. The buttons on his coat—shining gold skulls—bright enough to blind. Lucifer was dressed to wreak destruction and to take back what was his.

Once I find my wench.

Lounging in a club chair, sipping brandy with a casualness Lucifer envied—because the sin of coveting came so easily to him—Neptune listened to him rant. "Really, Lucifer, why all this fuss over a woman? One would almost think you cared about the chit."

"Of course I care! I care that someone dared spite me. The nerve of the bastard, kidnapping my fiancée. This kind of travesty cannot go unpunished." Left unsaid was the fact that he harbored a fondness for his wench and missed her.

"Or, you could look at it from the perspective that this Nemo fellow did you a favor. I mean, really, the devil getting married? Agreeing to monogamy? What happened to the guy I knew back in the Dark Ages who used to indulge in orgies with the witch covens that summoned him?"

What happened to that devil? He'd gotten tired of being alone. As if he'd ever tell this pompous ass something that made him seem so weak. "You're looking at this all wrong, old friend. What better torture is there than to be bound to one woman for eternity? What greater sin is there than to withhold my incredible erotic skills and massive dick from females everywhere?"

"Only you would see it that way."

"That is because I am all seeing and all knowing."

"I thought that was your brother."

Lucifer scowled. "Just because God coined that phrase first doesn't mean he's got exclusive rights to it."

"So what are you going to try next, given you can't sense where she is at all?"

What indeed? He couldn't kill what he couldn't find.

Lucifer's hellphone quacked as it announced an incoming text message—not to be confused with the new hex messages the witches were playing around with. Hex by Text. Lucifer funded their Kick-In-The-Ass-Starter fund and was, so far, loving the chaos the easy-to-send hexes were causing.

He glanced at his screen.

The water levels in the wilds are rising again.

Dammit. He'd rather hoped they'd stabilized. Holding the barrier around the ninth ring was taxing his magical defenses. Poor Nefertiti, his personal sorceress of the last few centuries, was running out of males to screw. Sex-based magic was powerful, but greedy.

How much longer could he stem the tide threatening to wash Hell clean?

Help me.

The whispered plea tickled him, and he looked around with a frown. "Did you say something?" Lucifer asked Neptune.

"Nothing, but I will reiterate that you're wasting your time. Gaia's probably off fornicating with that bearded fellow."

"Gaia wouldn't cuckold me." Even if she had a long time ago done it to Neptune——*with me.* Back then, he and the sea god enjoyed a rivalry when it came to wenching. *I won.* Because once you tasted the devil, nothing else would do.

Luc.

Again that soft murmur came brushing against his senses, a delicate touch that could only belong to one woman.

His woman.

Lucifer clutched at that fragile green thread, a thread that led from Hell to the mortal plane.

Time to go.

He didn't bother excusing himself with Neptune. That would be much too polite. Nor did he give the sea god any warning as he slashed his hand down and ripped open a portal between Hell and Earth.

As briny water gushed through the crack, Lucifer stepped through the doorway he created into chaos.

What fun.

Raging seawater filled a large cavern dimly lit by some glowing orbs suspended from the ceiling. Within the liquid mess, a spinning vortex sucked, funneling the water within the cave straight into a portal that led to Hell.

Aha, so this is where that liquid mess is coming from.

Interesting, but not as interesting as his wench imprisoned within a cage suspended above the churning waves.

Unlike a certain princess he'd lusted after a few decades ago, she was wearing too much clothing. It occurred to him for a moment to dress her right, but then again, now wasn't the time for that particular fantasy, given he also wasn't wearing the right outfit. His favorite black cape was currently at the cleaners.

She'd yet to remark upon his charismatic presence. Perhaps she'd not heard the sound of his magnificence arriving. He would have to work on his attention-grabbing entrances, apparently.

"Wench! There you are. I've been looking everywhere for you!" he bellowed.

"Luc?" His name emerged as a whisper.

"Yes, it's me. Who else were you expecting, that upstart with the sub? I must say I'm a touch miffed with you, wench. How dare you try and skip out on our engagement by taking off with that scruffy, bearded fellow."

"He kidnapped me." She uttered this with a little more fire.

But not enough to suit him.

He made a tsking sound. "Don't you dare try to placate me by making excuses. Come down out of that cage this instant," he commanded.

"I can't."

"Are you defying me?" Usually, it was a turn-on, but in this instance, he was worried that she lacked her usual vigor when throwing his orders back in his face.

"I can't escape this cage."

Can't? That he had to see.

Walking on water, lest he get his authentic boots wet—his brother's kid wasn't the only one who could do great things—he made his way to Gaia. He frowned once he got close enough to study the bars entrapping her. "What is this cage made of?"

Lucifer asked, and yet, he instantly guessed as soon as the words left his mouth. How could he not recognize the sinful human waste that tingled his fingers when he touched the bars? But while he might find radioactive waste a pleasant drug for his senses, he knew Gaia was highly allergic.

Someone had discovered her weakness and exploited it.

Usually, Lucifer would applaud that type of deviousness, but given it affected his wench, which in turn affected him—because a blue-balled devil was an unhappy devil—it was unacceptable.

"I can't escape the pollution, Luc. It's killing me."

Never. While Lucifer might allow the mortals to poison the Earth, he always made sure it wasn't enough to cause permanent damage. Some might mistakenly call it doing something nice for his wench, but he called it making sure she didn't claim a headache when he wanted sex.

"Is this your way of saying you want my help? I might be convinced for a price." He leered at her through the bars, refusing to allow worry to show in his gaze. The Lord of Hell did not worry. He also did not rescue, but if a certain lady asked, and promised a favor, well then, he was all about the bargain.

"Are you going to make me beg?" Eyes dull with weariness met his for a moment.

"If you want, or you can offer sexual favors. I'm open to suggestions." He waggled his brows, hoping she went for the latter.

If anything, she seemed even more crushed. Her shoulders rounded as she sighed. "If I must. I guess it was too much to hope you'd save me just because you care."

Blast her. He hated it when she tugged at his emotions. People called him evil, and yet, was there truly anything more devious than a woman who knew how to make a devil dance to her tune?

Before she could promise or beg, or fellate him through the bars, Lucifer gripped the metal—enjoyed the cheap thrill as the radiation tingled his skin—and wrenched the rods apart. His impressive feat of strength didn't generate any applause. His wench still sat slumped.

Reaching in, he plucked Gaia from the toxic metal and cradled her in his arms. He even whispered, "Fear no longer. I've got you, wench." While the nasty taste of heroism tainted his palate, the cleansing fire of rage soon erased it.

Someone dared to harm my wench. Laying a finger on Gaia, his future queen, was akin to slapping him and declaring war.

Who knew having a fiancée would result in such fun?

Perhaps he could suggest she get kidnapped more often so he could go on a killing rampage and keep his skills toned.

Of course, rampaging worked better with an opponent.

As Lucifer stood atop the waves, he surveyed the chamber but saw nobody he could decimate. "Where is that miscreant who dared steal my woman and harm her?"

Limp in his arms, Gaia revealed rare weakness as she lay her head on his shoulder. "I don't know where he is. But I do know Adexios and Valaska were sucked into that whirlpool portal. However, I don't know where they ended up."

"It leads to Hell." He could feel the link to his plane through the rip. It was probably how Gaia had managed to reach out to him.

"Shouldn't we follow them and give them our aid?"

Damn her selfless—yet luscious—hide. "Not yet. First you need to visit your garden and refresh yourself."

"Are you saying I don't look pretty?" She lifted her head to regard him with sultry green eyes that never failed to enthrall him. Gaia might be currently as weak as a newborn hellkitten, but with just one look, she was able to control him.

I am under her command.

Damn her. Damn him. Damn them both to Hell—where he had a king-sized bed they liked to spend a lot of time in. Naked, of course.

"Wench, you could wear a burlap sack, roll in a dung pile, and shave your head. I would still find you attractive. Your annoyingly inherent beauty shines through no matter what your exterior appearance." Ugh. How grotesque. Attracted to her for more than her body? The horror of it.

"Why, Luc, that was almost poetic," she said, unable to hide her utter shock.

"I know. I am totally grossed out, too," he said, wrinkling his nose. "Before I lose my breakfast, what do you say we get out of here? First stop, the Garden of Life, next stop, a showdown with Nemo, where you can have a front row seat as I pull out his innards." Then strangle him with them. But no need to give away the entire surprise.

Soft lips nuzzled his neck. "I don't suppose we have time for a maiden to show her hero how grateful she is?"

"There's always time for sinful pleasures. But first, I have a tiny matter to take care of. This unauthorized rip offends me."

I wonder what's on the other side keeping it open?

Who cared? He just hoped they liked Hell-roasted barbecue.

A negligent toss of his hand tossed a fireball that veered, much like a heat-seeking missile. The giant flaming sphere dove down into the heart of the whirlpool, arrowing for a certain portal.

One matter taken care of—and, no, he didn't need to hear and see the boom to know he'd just caused serious damage—he sketched a doorway to a certain garden. However, before he stepped through, the devil glared at the ceiling, where a certain broken cage still dangled.

This offends me. This was a reminder someone had hurt what was his.

Smoke sifted from his nostrils. The fires of Hell burned within him. He narrowed his gaze and aimed that rage, an invisible missile of pure force.

A rumble from above.

Time to go.

As Lucifer stepped through the portal into the disgustingly pleasant garden his wench called home, the groaning of shifting stone made his teeth vibrate. A few giant chunks shifted loose and fell with a giant plop. Another power wave came from below, his fireball hitting its target, spewing upwards a geyser of water. As chaos erupted, Lucifer snapped the portal shut before any of the dust and debris came through.

Mother Nature hated it when people dirtied her garden. Lucky for him, though, she didn't mind a certain devil making her dirty.

He made sure to bring that sparkle back to her eyes. He drew forth that gratingly cute and husky laugh of hers. He made her scream and call his name, and to truly blow her mind, he whispered against her lips, "I missed you."

Three emasculating words, but she took his shriveled pride, blew on it, and made it worth his while.

Best part of all, he got to keep his boots on. Fist pump!

Chapter Seventeen

"Always pay attention to your surroundings lest you lose an eye." Advice from One-Eyed Henrietta after the drunken archery incident.

For the second time in as many days, Valaska found herself spat up onto a beach. The gritty brown sand abraded her skin while the hazy sky cast a pall over everything.

What a change from their previous jungle paradise.

But at least we're closer to home. While she didn't recognize her location, she did note the familiar scent, if faint, of brimstone and ash. What was out of place was the odd machine hum.

Rolling to her knees, she grimaced as the sand clung to her skin and chafed. Nakedness was all well and good, especially when teasing a certain geeky partner, but in this gray damp, with the sensation that eyes watched her, she would have felt better with some clothes on.

She cast a quick glance around, looking for signs of trouble. No attacking frogmen. A shame. Nothing like an ambush to get sluggish blood moving.

Speaking of ambush, a quick peek behind showed nothing more pressing than sullen waves rolling in to shore. The same waves she'd wager that had carried her and Dex to this place as she vaguely recalled.

"Where are we?" groaned Dex as he came to his knees alongside her.

"Back in Hell, I think, but nowhere I've ever been."

By some miracle, Dex had managed to keep his glasses as well as his pack. Having not had time to dress in all their recent perils, she noted his skin also wore a layer of grit. A pity they didn't have time for a swim.

Squinting through his damp lenses, Dex peered around. "What is that noise? It sounds like a coal-fired train."

Chug. Chug. Chug.

Getting to her feet, senses still attuned to any sudden movement around them, Valaska pivoted in a full circle before stopping and facing seaward. She'd not initially noted the odd contraption in the water, given it sat several yards out. But now that she saw it, she couldn't help but stare at it.

"What is that?" she asked. Appearing like a giant-sized stove, it had a big metal belly, a steaming chimney, and a bevy of gears embedded in its sides. She'd never seen the like.

"That is supposed to be an impossibility," Dex muttered as he dropped his pack and waded toward the contraption.

She grabbed her sword before she followed, curiosity and apprehension invading her in equal measures. Machines notoriously didn't work in Hell, not without lots of magical help.

As for a contraption sitting in the sea, without anyone to man it? That pushed the boundaries of strange even for Hell.

"What is it?" she asked as she got closer and felt the fine hairs on her skin rise. The magic exuding from the thing electrified the air. This close she could see that what she'd mistaken for gears from afar were actually runes. These mystical carvings turned and churned, their purpose unclear until she and Dex waded farther in and reached the front of it.

A portal hung in the air before the machine, perfectly round and large. Larger than anything she'd ever seen, and even more astonishing, it wasn't shrinking or snapping shut.

Portals took a lot of power. Most individuals couldn't even call one for themselves, let alone open and maintain one of this size.

And as to the purpose? From it spewed water, briny seawater.

"Unbelievable," Dex muttered.

"I think we just found the answer as to how the water got here."

Dex shook his head. "The water yes, but what we still don't know is, who is responsible for this magical contraption and why? Why flood the wilds?"

"Didn't Gaia say something about running into a fellow named Nemo?"

"Yes. And a machine like this could definitely be something he might have designed or helped build. However, the magic…" Dex paused and returned to peer at the sides where the glyphs spun. "Even if someone had the knowledge to create this kind of intricacy, no one has this much magic to spare."

"Not even Lucifer?"

"He might be able to do something like this for a few minutes, but this…" Dex placed his hand on the metal side and sucked in a breath. "This is not natural."

Valaska couldn't help but roll her eyes. "Obviously. It's made of shaped metal."

"I'm not talking about the machine itself, but the magic. There's a taint to it." He snatched his hand back. "Give me your sword."

She clutched it closer. "Why do you want my

blade? There is no enemy." Was there? She peeked around in case she'd missed something.

Nobody approached. She tried not to let her dejection show.

"I need your sword so I can pry open the latch at the front."

Latch? What latch?

She let him borrow her blade as she followed Dex back to the front of the big stove thing. Distracted by the portal before, which she noted now seemed to waver around the edges, she paid more attention to the actual machine and noted a square inset within the belly. The square sported hinges at one end and a latch at the other, indicating some kind of opening into the machine.

Dex lifted her blade and brought the pommel down on the latch.

"Why don't you just slide it open?" she asked.

"It's got magic holding it locked."

She couldn't help but raise a brow. "You do realize you can't break magic by pummeling it?" She should know. She'd tried more than once before admitting defeat. Magical locks needed magical keys, or locksmiths, to open them.

"Ah, but here's the thing. I have just enough power to focus on your sword hilt."

"You're using my blade as a magical hammer?" The shame.

Bang. Pop. "Yes," he said, turning to her, one hand holding the sword down by his side while the other pushed his glasses back up.

"What's in there?" she asked, reaching for the blade that he handed over without question. She stroked it. *Fear not, my precious sword. We'll soon erase the humiliation of being used as a common tool with blood.*

"I have a sneaky suspicion about what's inside,"

Dex said. "But I am hoping I'm wrong."

A tug on the door to the machine opened it and without even an ominous creak to signal evil portent. And if ever there was a device that deserved one…

At the sight within, Valaska couldn't help but suck in a breath. "What the fuck is going on in there?"

"Say hello to the batteries that run the machine."

She blinked, and despite her oftentimes-hard heart, couldn't help but feel pity. "Batteries? But those are demons."

Indeed, packed inside the contraption were at least a few dozen demons, their limbs shackled above their heads in chains. Horned heads hung low, skin sagged, their color dull, and, in some cases, sore riddled. Not one of the demonic beings showed any signs of life, even as gray light flooded the space.

"Are they dead?" she asked, letting her sword dip forward to poke one in its belly. Not even a twitch to show it felt it.

"Not yet, but they will be and soon. If my hypothesis is correct, then the manacles holding these demons provides a direct hookup to this machine. When the machine is activated, the demons' magic is siphoned and used to open a portal to the mortal side."

"But there's so many of them," Valaska said.

"Because the amount of magic needed to maintain the portal requires it. I think this discovery explains why we didn't find any demons in the wild." Although she had to wonder how they crammed the bigger ones inside. And where were the bodies of the dead ones?

Did it really matter? Let Lucifer's scientist unravel that mystery.

"I guess this thing explains the dying demon we found." Valaska backed away from the machine as the skin on the yellow bile demon in the front began to ooze pus from a spot that appeared on its chest. The flesh bubbled.

And still the demon didn't twitch.

It was horrifying to the extreme.

"We have to do something," she exclaimed.

"You're right, we do." With that, Dex slammed the door shut.

"What are you doing? Shouldn't we be freeing them or something?" she asked.

Dex stepped in front of her when she would have opened the door. Sporting a grim expression, he shook his head. "These demons are too far gone. You would only be delaying the inevitable. Also, if you enter the chamber while the machine is still running, then it will start siphoning your life force and magic as well."

"So what can we do then?"

"What we need to do is ensure no others join them."

"But how?" She banged the tip of her blade off the machine, the metal clang louder than its chugging. "I can't exactly chop it to bits."

"By getting it to explode."

"You have more bombs?" She couldn't help a lilt of excitement. Who didn't like a loud explosion?

"Not quite. But a pressurized reaction doesn't need chemicals."

Once again, Dex and the weird workings of his mind were lost on her, so she stood and watched his trim buttocks as he ran to the beach. He dropped to his knees alongside his pack and began scrounging. He tossed a few things from it on the sand before jogging back. As he reached her, he said, "Give me a boost, would you?"

Instead of asking why, she did as he asked, cupping her hands together so that he could step on them. She propelled him upwards until he could toss his bag atop the machine. Then he gripped the edge of the giant stove and vaulted over.

This close she couldn't see a thing, so she stepped away from the machine and craned her head.

The chimney proved taller than Dex, but only by a few feet. What emitted from the top of the pipe didn't bear any color unlike smoke, and yet it did expel something. She could see the hazy disruption.

"What is that coming out of the pipe?" she asked.

"I don't think it has a name because I don't think it's been done before. And yet, many have theorized about it. If I'm correct, then we're seeing the results of an esoteric reaction. In other words, what you get when a demon, or other living being's life force, is changed into magic."

Smoke in other words. Demon smoke.

As he shimmied up the chimney, bag looped over one shoulder, she grasped his plan.

Sure enough, he stuffed his handy backpack in the hole at the top, providing a seal. While the pressure and the magical heat would build, the sturdily made bag, reinforced with its own brand of magic, wouldn't disintegrate easily.

No sooner had he blocked the pipe than the machine took on a hum that grew in pitch.

"Get away from it," Dex yelled as he slid down the chimney.

Run away and leave her partner behind? Did he know that little about Amazons?

She waited for him.

Legs flailing, as he ran on air for extra distance, Dex leaped off the machine and landed in the sandy surf with an "Ooomph."

Creak. Metal groaned as a tremor shook the contraption, and a peek behind Valaska's shoulder showed the portal wobbling.

But that wasn't the most worrisome part. "Did a fireball just shoot out of the portal?"

"Yes."

She didn't need to ask if he saw said fiery meteor stop in mid air, shiver, and then begin shooting back toward the vibrating machine, or was it looking for them?

Either way, it didn't matter.

"Stop staring and run," Dex admonished as he grabbed her free hand and pulled her toward the beach.

Together they dashed, even as the whine from the giant stove pitched higher and higher.

The fireball, though, proved silent.

Until it hit.

With an un-hell-ly scream, and a wail of bursting metal, the machine exploded with a bang that shook Hell and blasted a shockwave.

Valaska couldn't stop herself from falling, the hard jostle into the wet sand making her lose her grip on her sword. Hands free, she covered the most vulnerable part of her, her head, but a side glance had her eyes widening as she noted Dex cupping his groin instead of his cranium.

With bits of sand, droplets of seawater, and metal chunks dropping all around them, she closed her eyes and lost sight of him.

Slowly, insanity receded to quiet.

No more hum.

The machine was gone, and she lived.

But what of Dex?

It wasn't her partner that answered. "You fools broke my portal device."

The voice wasn't one she knew, and that meant she'd gotten caught off guard.

Again.

The shame made her cringe. While the echo of the blast still rang in her ears, that wasn't an excuse for not spotting the intruder who'd sneaked up on them.

Lifting her head, she spotted her sword and, without even thinking, lunged for it, only to see it snatched by a webbed hand.

Rising to her knees, Valaska glared at the frogman who held her precious blade. Yet, Mr. Green and Webbed wasn't the biggest threat. That was reserved for the bearded fellow in front of her, aiming a gun at them both.

"Nemo, I suppose?" she surmised, given she doubted there were many bearded fellows wandering around. Lucifer tended to set trends—by killing those who didn't follow his lead. "So nice of you to come find us. We've been looking for you."

"So I heard. I see you escaped the island my minions were holding you prisoner on. A pity, you would have made sturdy power sources for the device."

"Sorry to disappoint. You should get together with my dad sometime. I disappoint him all the time, too." Dex shrugged and smile. "It's why I'm the favored son."

"I thought you were an only son," Valaska said.

"I am."

"Stop with this pointless chatter." Nemo glared over the barrel of his weapon. "If you escaped, then where is Gaia?"

Valaska felt a moment's chagrin that she'd not given Mother Earth a second thought since they'd arrived in this strange place.

Did she make it out? Or had she drowned in the

rising water before they shut the portal?

Not knowing what happened to Gaia didn't mean Valaska couldn't lie about it.

Except Dex beat her to it and told a whopper. "She's gone to get reinforcements. Any minute now, she's going to arrive with Lucifer and his legion to rescue us and put an end to you."

Damn him for stealing this great opportunity to earn points with the boss. And damn him more for his lack of faith in her abilities to save his ass.

Offended, she retorted, "Hold on a second, Dex. I am perfectly capable of hogtying this dumbass myself, probably having time to shave the bird's nest on his chin and present him to Lucifer. Why he'll probably thank me for saving you both."

"Lucifer thank us?" Dex made a face. "You have met him, right? By the time he's done with the press, he'll have singlehandedly captured Nemo, saved Hell, and gotten the girl."

"You're both deluded. Lucifer has already lost the battle. It's too late for him, and you, and everyone in Hell. Even if you destroyed one device, it matters not. The plan is in motion, and nothing, not even my death, can stop it."

"I don't suppose you'd mind if I tested that theory?" Valaska asked. "Then again, screw asking. Why don't I just kill you and see what happens?"

She finished her words with a lunge. The wet sand shifted underfoot, and she stumbled, only a fraction but enough for Nemo to turn his body, raise his thigh, and knock her back.

Before she could recover, his gun was only a foot away from Valaska's forehead. "I am done talking to you. Originally, I had thought to save you both as more power for the machine, but now that you've broken it, and proven so troublesome, I no longer have a need for either of you."

Did he really think the gun scared her? Nemo was obviously still new to the rules in Hell. Firearms, much like electronics, were hit and miss in the pit, the magic and esoteric forces making them unreliable. The gun was just as likely to blow up in his face as fire a bullet.

Thing was the probability was fifty-fifty, which meant… *This might hurt.*

But Valaska didn't fear pain. She stared at Nemo and dared him to fire.

Trust Dex to rely on words instead of violence for answers. "Now let's not act too rashly here. Dead is so final. Think about it. How do you know we won't still be useful down the line? You do know who I am, don't you?"

"I do. Charon's son. Devil-son to Lucifer. A cosseted male with high connections. Perhaps I should keep you as leverage."

A wry smile twisted Dex's lips. "If you're thinking of ransoming, then you don't know my dad too well. He wouldn't spare any of his wealth to free me. He's old school and thinks a boy should solve his own problems and not buy his way out of them. And I wouldn't suggest dangling me in front of my mother. She goes a little cuckoo when her baby boy is threatened. She kicks some serious ass."

Feeling a little miffed that he sounded so obviously impressed by his mother, Valaska snapped, "We don't need your mommy to help us. I already told you I'm perfectly capable of saving your ass myself."

Dex tossed her a smile and a wink. "I know you are, but if we let my mom come to the rescue, she'll probably bring snacks."

Ignoring her gurgling tummy didn't mean nobody else heard.

Nemo's gun didn't waver in its aim, even as he rolled his eyes. "And my boss thought taking over Hell would prove a challenge. Not likely with idiots such as you leading the charge."

"Idiot?" Dex drew himself straight, and a hard glint entered his eye. "I'll have you know I shamed my entire lineage by graduating with honors."

"And yet all those smarts still saw you washed up on my beach. Enough talk. You, I'll keep because I might have a use for you, but the girl, she's useless to me."

She stared into the dark barrel of the gun, only now noting the tiny glyphs of magic inscribed on it. *Damn.* The odds had just changed, and not for the better. Yet Valaska didn't flinch.

She didn't fear playing the roulette of life.

Except Dex apparently didn't like the odds. He stepped in front of her.

She stepped to the side, but he followed. He seemed determined to shield her with his body. If she weren't so touched by his bravery, she would have ripped him a new one for treating her like a weak girl.

Still, though, she was the warrior in this relationship. It was up to her to fight.

"What do you think you are doing?" she asked.

He didn't look at her as he replied. "I like you too much to allow this fictional character to end your life."

"Does this feel fictional to you?" Nemo snarled, pressing the barrel of the gun to the lens on Dex's glasses. She wanted to go around him, but his arms extended, and damn those wiry ferryman pipes, she couldn't slip around.

"I got this, brat."

"Brat?" She crossed her arms over her chest and decided to let him do his thing. She could always avenge his death after. "Well, excuse me for trying to do what I've been trained to."

"Punish me later," Dex said. "And there will be a later because I'm sure even Captain Nemo wouldn't shoot a guy with glasses."

Cocking back the hammer, Nemo let an evil smirk pull his lips. "Guess again."

Bang.

Chapter Eighteen

"These robes are guaranteed to resist the puncture of even the sharpest of monster teeth." One of the key features learned during the four-hour infomercial on the latest Ferryman Uniform.

The recoil was only somewhat worse than the deafening explosion so close to his ears. Adexios staggered from the recoil.

Oh, and for those wondering, he was alive, and not bleeding from a giant hole in his head.

See, Adexios knew most guns were just as likely to fire as misfire. Mechanics without magic just wasn't that reliable. He knew that was what Valaska was counting on, that and that her luck would hold.

But Adexios couldn't let her survival rest on chance. *Not when I love her so much.*

And he did, love her that was. It wasn't until that moment when he realized he might lose her that the truth gobsmacked him.

Funny how love also drew the hero out of him. It was easy, so easy to place himself as a shield before her. When Nemo placed the gun against his glasses, Adexios almost laughed.

Because, as Nemo soon discovered, he wasn't kidding when he said his mom had gotten him the sturdiest glasses around.

The gun fired, hit his lens, and ricocheted, right back to its sender.

As Nemo gasped, probably because the bullet left a hole in his shoulder that bled profusely, Adexios staggered, the impact of the bullet against his glasses still rather substantial.

Valaska grabbed him and gave him a shake—an I-care shake that almost gave him whiplash. "You fucking idiot. What did you do that for?" An admonishment followed by a kiss on his lips.

Not a long kiss, a short passion-filled one ending with a whispered, "We'll finish this later."

Because first they had to fight.

Again?

The old Adexios would have sighed and complained about having to exert himself. The new him, known as a very dashing Dex, found himself adrenalized by the prospect. While Valaska ran at the frogman with her sword, Dex dodged the other two that jabbed their tongues his way.

Nemo, holding a hand to his bleeding shoulder, screamed, "Kill them."

"Are you talking to them," Dex asked, "Or us? You know, just so it's clear."

"Die!" Given Nemo aimed the gun at Dex, he got his answer.

Bang. The gun fired. However, a little too angry to take proper aim meant Nemo's missile didn't quite hit its intended target.

Down went one of Nemo's allies.

Wait, make that two, as Valaska managed to wrestle her sword from the frogman, who now lay twitching on the sand in a spreading green puddle.

Two down, and quite a few more to go.

As the frogmen grouped together and formed a barrier, Nemo fled to the jungle.

As he and Valaska put themselves back-to-back

on the beach, their gazes intent on the enemy, it occurred to Dex he should say something. "So, um, it looks like we might die."

"With glory."

"And blood," he added, the Amazon words he'd heard on the reality show coming to his lips. "But before we send our spirits to be reborn, I thought I should tell you that this whole adventure, and getting to know you and stuff, has been great."

Feeling awkward about his admission, Adexios ducked and grabbed a piece of driftwood on the beach. Not a big piece but enough he could help bat away some of the tongues trying to get fresh with him and Valaska.

"Can't we talk about this later?" Valaska muttered as she twirled her blade, slicing at the tongues that dared dart toward them.

But what if there wasn't a later? He found his courage, which oddly enough was in his heart and not his balls. "I don't want to wait anymore. Valaska, I love you." There. He'd said it. A pity he wouldn't live long enough for her to punish him for it.

"Me, too. Now shut up with this feelings crap while I get rid of these froggies."

Dex would have liked to stand and gape stupidly for a moment as her words sank in.

Me, too? As in me too she loved him?

Except he couldn't get her to clarify because some stupid frogs were determined to kill them both before he could ask.

Hell no.

Whack. Swing. *Thump.* His many years as a ferryman, dealing with troublesome sea monsters, meant Adexios had a firm grasp of how to wield a staff.

Mind you, the driftwood staff he held had rough edges and a pointed tip instead of a being shaped like a paddle, but that served his purpose quite well, as it meant instead of an oomph when he caught them in the belly, it was a gurgling "Argh." A deadly argh.

In that moment, Adexios was elevated from simple Ferryman to Ferrywarrior. Cool. Wait until he told his dad.

Adrenaline running high, he and Valaska danced on the beach, a deadly pair—in love—wielding their weapons and meting out death. It was the most coordinated he'd ever been, and when they finished their graceful duet, they found themselves, face to face, amidst the carnage.

Panting slightly, yet both alive. Unharmed, if slimed.

He didn't say anything as they stared at each other, just grabbed her face and pulled her toward him, claiming her mouth.

Yes, claiming.

There were few things he felt strong about in life, but this woman, having her in his life, his arms, his bed? That brought out the beast in him.

Or at least the dictator.

"We. Should be. Going to. Find Nemo," she gasped between kisses.

"In a second," he growled. "I want to hear you say it first."

"Say what?"

He wrapped his fist in her hair and tugged her head back so he could nibble the smooth column of her neck. "You know what I want."

She reached down and grabbed him, her grip firm around his erect cock. "I'd say that was pretty obvious."

He nipped her skin, a firm bite that would leave a mark. She moaned.

"Say it," he murmured against her skin before lapping at it.

"Fine. I love you, too, but can we get to all this sappy stuff after we're done?"

"Now that I know there's an after, you can have whatever you want." Dex released her and was gratified at her small mewl of disappointment. With a slap on her ass, he headed toward the jungle. "Coming?" he asked over his shoulder.

Another smile stretching her lips, Valaska strode after him. "I hope so. My pussy could use a tongue-lashing. So let's get this done quickly."

Dex's momentary grace lapsed at her words, and he stumbled. She chuckled as she swept past him.

Once they entered the jungle, following the well-worn trail within the shadowy boughs, they stopped talking. The jungle itself proved abnormally quiet. Not even the hum of insects or chirp of birds broke the silence.

If not for the fresh trail of blood they followed, Adexios might have thought them alone.

The jungle itself didn't prove very big. In short order, they'd cleared the quiet depths and found themselves at the bottom of a small mountain, the sides ridged and seamed, as if the rock had melted, hardened, then cracked.

"This is a volcano," Adexios noted. "But I don't think it's been active in a while." Not given the plants struggling to grow through the cracks.

"Dead or not, we're going in it. The blood trail goes that way." Valaska pointed a finger at the base of the volcano, where a dark shadowy entrance practically screamed, Do Not Enter.

So, of course, what did they do?

They entered. The interior of the tunnel proved

dark and cool after the stifling damp of the jungle. It appeared of natural construction, a molten stone river frozen in twisted lines.

They couldn't see if any blood spotted the floor, but they ran to the other end, the gray beacon of light their guide.

He didn't need Valaska's outstretched arm to know he should slow down before popping out.

Who knew what might await them?

Pausing, they listened.

Not a sound broke the silence. Not even a gurgle of a frogman, the inhalation of a breath, the flutter of some feathers.

On tiptoe, they inched to the opening, one to each side. Without asking, he poked his head out, hoping he wouldn't have it exploded like a melon.

When nothing happened, he remembered to open his eyes and look around.

There wasn't much to see.

The interior of the volcano was shaped like a hollow bowl. The high ridges went up almost straight, but at the base, it widened out, and amongst the lumped and twisted rock, life tried to grow.

But that wasn't the most interesting thing. In the midst of the hollowed bottom was a body of water, surrounded by dark sand and, bobbing in it, a submarine.

But not any submarine, a giant purple one with a painted eye and metal rakes on the prow as teeth.

Cool.

He would have dearly loved to explore the sub, but that wasn't the only item of note in the valley. A few yards away, by the side of the lake, sat a jungle hut made of bamboo logs, lashed together with vines and thatched with leaves. How Robinson Crusoe.

"Come out, come out, wherever you are!"

Valaska sang.

He shot her a look. "What are you doing? What happened to surprising the enemy?"

"One, it wouldn't be sporting. And two…" She shrugged. "He knows we're coming. He knows I'm going to kill him. Maybe he'll take it like a man."

If by a man she meant standing on his sub wielding a rather large machine gun, one with runes inscribed on its barrel.

Dex was starting to find himself envious of the other man's toys. Envious, but not stupid. "Take cover," Dex yelled, even as he knew it was too late. Still, though, he dove in front of Valaska as the gun began to chatter, expelling its deadly bullets.

Lying atop Valaska on the sand, he ignored her grumbled, "Get off me, you idiot," and waited to get ripped to shreds by bullets.

Except he didn't die.

Neither of them did.

A warm breeze, heavily scented of flowers, interspersed with the heavier pungent odor of sulfur and Old Spice filled the air.

Help had arrived.

Chapter Nineteen

"Blow something up. It's a great stress reliever."
Lucifer's philosophy on most anything that bothers him.

Stepping forth from the portal, Lucifer held his wench's hand and took instant note of the action. For those obsessed with exact details—*How did you know where to go?*—he'd pinpointed the coordinates using HPS tracking on Adexios' Hellphone. Not up to date on Hell's latest technology? HPS stood for the Hell Positioning System.

Of course, Lucifer's use of the coordinates with his magic didn't always translate perfectly, hence why he found himself a few degrees off course.

But those few degrees meant perfection, as he found himself arriving just as a battle commenced.

And no one invited me!

Funny thing considering Adexios and that Amazon wench were both about to get turned into Swiss cheese—the authentic kind, not that dairy creation on the mortal plane—and yet hadn't bothered to give him a shout.

Adexios was turning out to be a hog when it came to excitement and adventure. Time to remind him who was boss—and was the undefeated champion when it came to killing those who threatened his rule. Although Muriel was doing her best to catch up. A good thing he was somewhat fond of her, or she'd have visited the abyss a while ago.

Lucifer couldn't quite dump Charon's kid in a bottomless hole—damned friendship! However, he did intend to a talk with that boy, and that would probably work better if Adexios was alive for it.

That Nemo is turning into a pain in my ass. The kind without lube. He thinks he's going to kill more of my people? I think not.

With a stare that surely reflected the fires of hell—something numerous painters had yet to properly convey in portrait—Lucifer batted the bullets to the ground.

However, before he turned his attention to the gun turret, Gaia said, in a firm voice that never failed to delight him, especially when she used it to give him orders in the bedroom, "Let me take care of Nemo. I think your prowess will be needed elsewhere."

"You mean you want me to go off and bang someone? I thought that was a major no-no."

"Not that prowess," Gaia growled. "Your fighting one. Take a look over there."

Letting his gaze follow her pointed finger, Lucifer caught his breath in delight. It seemed he would get that battle he'd hoped for. From the waters that lapped against the bobbing sub poured forth monsters and beasts, the likes of which he'd never seen. Two-legged frogmen, giant-sized crabs, and was that the tentacles of a kraken waving in there? Surely that watery lagoon was too small to hold them all, but explain that to the monsters that erupted in a wave and headed for the shore.

Adexios and Valaska wisely retreated to stand by them.

Somewhat mollified that they'd bowed to his superior skill, he decided not to feed them to the hellodiles in his moat.

"Where are those things coming from?" Lucifer asked, even as he knew it had to be a portal. An unauthorized one. "These creatures do not belong here." And he was totally wearing the wrong outfit for the occasion. He'd put on his uniform, with a few casual touches to remind Nemo who got to get between Gaia's thighs.

Me and only me.

Dressed to impress, Lucifer had only expected to deal with the bearded fellow who called himself a captain, and yet, judging by the approaching crustacean wave, he should have worn his clamming outfit. His thigh-high waders had been made by the same company as his slicker. The duckies appeared magnificent on his boots and, even better, were also found embroidered on the suspenders that held the waders up.

"There's got to be a portal somewhere," Adexios announced.

Too late. I already thought it.

Valaska pointed to the rustic hut. "I'll bet they've got the portal machine inside that hut."

"Come on, let's go blow it up." Adexios grasped the Amazon's hand—who, in a surprise move, allowed it instead of chopping the appendage off. The pair ran to the hut, but some of the crab creatures scuttled to block their way.

"Hey, get back over here," Lucifer yelled. "You're supposed to be my fight." He didn't let his minions fight alone.

What Valaska didn't decimate with her sword, Lucifer grabbed with power and flung. Even Adexios joined the battle, swinging a stick.

Whee! Lucifer was having a grand time flinging the creatures around. Until he realized the wave seemed never ending. He began to conserve some of his magic.

Even an omnipotent demon had his limits.

As did a certain goddess.

Slowing down meant he took a peek over at his wench, who'd kept herself busy.

Vines extended from the jungle, long green ropy strands that bound Nemo against his gun turret. But that wasn't all his show-off fiancée did. Expending a chunk of magic, she'd animated some trees, her new favorite trick ever since that damned movie with the hobbit. She let out a giggle when the leafy warriors uprooted themselves and stomped into the fray.

Her treemen, though, couldn't take the place of real warriors, and they lacked the numbers to fight the horde.

"I need my army," Lucifer grumbled.

"Or an explosion," Gaia mumbled, toeing the ground beneath her bare foot—with its dainty toes painted a light pink.

"Are you hiding a bomb under those skirts, wench?" She certainly had a trigger between her thighs for getting him to blow.

"Kiss me," she asked him.

"Now?" He flicked a wave of power at the encroaching sea monsters.

"Yes, now, and don't hold back," she added, grabbing him by the lapels and yanking him close.

Debauchery in the midst of battle? He was good with that.

Lucifer slanted his mouth over hers, loving the crisp sweet and yet tart flavor of her lips, much like green apples at harvest.

As he wrapped his arms around her, he pulled her plump frame against him and explored the seam of her mouth with his tongue.

She parted her lips, and he deepened the kiss.

Sharp teeth nipped at his lower lip.

How he wanted her. Here and now. But outside forces distracted him. He waved his hand, batting away a crab that dared think to interfere.

"Don't stop, Luc. I need you. I want you," Gaia whispered against his lips whilst her hands cupped him.

He didn't want to stop, but those blasted monsters wouldn't stop coming. It made him angry.

Wisps of smoke curled from his ears.

She slid a hand inside his pants and gripped him. Stroked him.

A tentacle dared wrap around his ankle.

"Take me," she whispered.

He wanted to. He burned for her. He *hungered.*

Yet, instead of lifting her skirts, he found himself forced to turn to deal with a distraction. He held out his hand, and a sword made of blazing hellfire appeared in it.

Hey, gorgeous. Long time, no see.

And for those who might grumble about his love for his weapon, Gaia was good with it. She'd only gotten a little jealous the time he'd brought his sword to bed. Now his blade watched from a chair.

Kissing the molten hilt, he smiled—a smile that had made the strong hearted tremble. A smile that had brought about ammonia lakes. A smile that said, "Hello, asshole. Prepare to die." Wielding his mighty sword with a skill none could compare, Lucifer smote a few of the daring beasts.

"Can't you see I'm busy?" he roared.

Apparently the monsters didn't see too well because they kept coming. Kept him busy. Kept him away from his wench's lips.

"We aren't done, *Luc.*" She purred his name. He knew that sound. That promise…

Impatience was one of his virtues. He growled as

he cleaved through the monsters keeping him from his greedy goal.

"That's it, my demon lover. Kill them. Kill them all. Then take me."

He'd take her all right. "Just a minute, wench, while I deal with the seafood part of our engagement dinner."

Lucifer continued to slice and dice, dodge and duck, wondering if his minions would ever find the damned portal and close it.

An explosion caused the ground to tremble, and the hut Adexios and Valaska had disappeared into burst into flaming bits.

But no sign of his minions. Had they perished?

Hmm. That might prove annoying to explain to Charon and his wife.

However, more annoying would be if the sea creatures, whose portal had just closed on whatever plane they'd come from, actually managed to take a bite out of the lord of Hell. The pincers closed on air, narrowly avoiding a pinch.

In his own words, *Hell no.* His gaze narrowed. Time to finish this. "Strip whilst I finish, wench. This won't take long."

In his mind, it was only the briefest moment to slash his way through the monsters. Being a bit of a busybody—a sin she just couldn't help—Gaia had some of her treemen helping.

But Lucifer made sure he acquitted himself well. By the time he was done, he stood thigh deep in seafood.

With nothing left to fight, he let his sword disappear. He brushed a hand down his military uniform, magically sluicing any seafood bits from the fabric before stepping into the air to avoid the steaming entrails.

Gaia met him, just past the carnage, still fresh as

a daisy. A pity, he preferred it when she put on her whorish rose red and pricked him with her thorns. But there was something to be said for gentle simplicity.

It made a leering demon want to ravage.

Except the pillaging and murdering wasn't quite done. "Shall we finish what we started?" Lucifer asked as he placed a kiss on her hand.

"Yes." She turned her green gaze onto Nemo, still trussed in vines, his dark eyes shooting daggers of hate.

Look at me, I made a new enemy. Such fun. A devil could never have too many. It kept a demon young staying ahead of enemy plots. Except this Nemo fellow wasn't the head honcho of the operation. Lucifer recognized a minion when he saw one.

Floating on a platform of air, he and Gaia stepped onto the sub—*my sub*—and approached the captain.

He didn't waste time. "Tell us who you work for," Lucifer demanded.

"Never. I'd rather die first."

"If you insist." It took but a thought to bring his sword back and send it swinging. The decapitated head of Nemo soared through the air, but before it could hit the water, a purple tentacle rose from the depths and snatched it.

"What did you do that for?" Gaia huffed. "Now how are we supposed to know who he works for?"

"I wasn't about to let him have a villain monologue. I coined those, you know, and now everyone with an agenda thinks they can use them. I say no. Besides, think of the fun we'll have finding out who's behind this. The best things in life don't come easily."

"You are warped, Luc."

"Very. But that twisted part of my dick is what

makes me such an awesome lover."

"Oh, I don't know. Maybe you should show me again."

"What about Charon's boy? Shouldn't we look for him and that girl he's smitten with?"

"I'm sure they're fine. That mother of his has had more leprechauns sacrificed to give him luck than I would have thought possible."

"True. And we do have more important matters to attend. I'll bet this sub has a bed."

"A bed? Look at you getting traditional with old age."

"Old?" Both his brows shot high. "I'll show you old, wench."

"Only if you catch me." With a giggle, Gaia dropped into the open hatch, and the devil followed.

And chased.

And debauched.

Numerous times.

Until they found a bed, which they used to sleep.

Chapter Twenty

"Live life to the fullest. You never know if it might be your last." From the Amazon teachings of Joan the Great.

As Valaska entered the hut, with Dex on her heels, it took a moment to adjust to the dimness. It also took a blink and second glance to realize that the inside was much, much larger than the outside.

"Bloody magic," she grumbled. Everywhere she turned, more magic. It irritated her because a sword and fist couldn't fight what she couldn't touch. "I knew I should have stayed on the beach and battled those crustaceans."

"Bitching already? You do know the boss can't hear you right now," Dex teased.

"I wasn't looking for brownie points. Just something to fight."

"Oh, I think you'll get your wish," Dex stated with certainty as they flowed from the first room, which held nothing but wooden crates, to the next.

"What makes you say that?" she asked.

No sooner had she spoken than a pair of frogmen rushed into the room, tongues whipping out. Awesome, she wasn't going to miss out on all the action.

Whirl. Slice. Dice. Jab.

Done.

Sigh.

Too easy.

Dex touched her on the arm, and she noted he had his head cocked. "Can you hear that?"

Since she doubted he meant the last dying gasps of the frogman at her feet, she listened and heard a familiar hum.

"Is that…"

He nodded. "Another one of those portal devices, which is where I'll wager those monsters from outside are coming from."

"We should totally check it out and smash it." Maybe kill a few creatures on the way.

Her step much lighter, she bounced through the current chamber, which held numerous bunks with rumpled bedding and a swampy smell.

They passed through two more chambers, one containing cages, empty ones, except for the a cell in the far corner, where a demon who'd not lived long enough to provide battery power, lay prone on the bottom.

A trio of frogmen came at them from a side corridor, waving more spears and giving them tongue. So rude on a first date.

It was also their last date.

She and Dex stepped over their bodies on their way to the next archway, from which the hum of the portal device seemed particularly loud.

Poking her head in, she noted no guards, surprising, given the machine loomed in the middle of the massive chamber, chugging away, powering its portal.

But this portal didn't lead to the mortal plane.

Who knew where this one went, but she would wager it wasn't a place anyone knew. From the glimmering rip between the planes lurched monsters of the aquatic kind. Iridescent skin glistened as the glowing orbs lighting the chamber reflected off the many-hued scales. Eerie, bulbous eyes stared unblinking.

Valaska dropped into a ready stance with her sword, and yet, even though some of the creatures glanced her way, none of them deviated from their trudging and slithering as they emptied from the portal rip and plopped into the lake alongside it.

"How much you want to bet that lake connects to the one outside in the volcano crater?" Dex mused aloud.

"I'll take that wager. If you're wrong, I get orgasmic oral. If you win, prepare for a mind-blowing BJ."

Dex gaped at her, and while his cheeks didn't turn red, his eyes did take on a bright glint. "I've never wanted to be more wrong."

"Never fear." She patted him on the cheek. "You're a man. It will happen sooner than later. Just not today I fear. It's a good thing I'm a grown woman who knows how to suck it up." She winked at him.

He swallowed. "Um, yeah, so ah, we need to blow up that machine," Dex stated unnecessarily.

"No shit. But with what?" This time they didn't have a handy backpack.

However, they did have lots of creatures.

Before she could explain her idea to Dex, she put it in motion. Did she plan to have fun while doing it? Hell yeah, which was why she raced at the aquatic beasts with a shrill battle cry. It drew the attention of a few.

She sliced through them with ease and, when they littered the hard, rocky ground, grabbed their twitching limbs and tossed them to the top of the device.

Having already caught on to her plan, Dex vaulted to the top of the machine and busied himself stuffing the chimney.

In no time at all, the pressure built, much like it had earlier with the device on the beach. While they didn't have the fireball of before, the whistle of demon smoke building, and the wobble of the portal, said it would blow soon.

"We have to go," she stated.

"Yes, but not out the front way. There's a tunnel back there. I think we should check it out." Dex stood atop the machine and pointed to the shadows lining the rear of the chamber.

She would have said no because she kind of wanted back outside fighting those sea monsters, except, before she could open her mouth, one of those shadows on the back wall twitched and then scattered.

Things that ran were automatic prey. "You are not escaping that easily," she muttered.

Valaska sprinted in the direction of the fleeing shape, Dex hot on her heels. She ducked through the crevice in the wall and found herself in another lava tunnel, just tall enough that she didn't have to crouch.

Ahead of them ran a figure clothed in a cloak that covered them head to foot. Man or woman? She couldn't tell and didn't care. Valaska pumped her legs harder and gained on the person.

Without even a quick glance back, the fleeing figure turned a corner and disappeared.

Much as she hated to slow down, Valaska halted before the edge and took a quick listen.

Not so Dex. "Don't let them get away."

Around the corner he bolted, and with a wry smile at his impetuousness, she followed, only to bump into him as he stood frozen before a portal.

"What are you waiting for? Jump before it closes."

"But we don't know where it goes." Dex hesitated.

A rumble shook the tunnel as rock dust sifted

down.

The device had exploded, and that meant their choice to run deeper into the mountain was proving exciting, as the tremble of the ground didn't stop. It continued. Fissures appeared in the walls. Silt rained on them, as did chunks of hardened lava.

The portal wobbled, its ragged edges shrinking. Given the choice of possibly getting crushed by a ton of rock or the unknown…

She grabbed Dex by the arm and shoved him through before stepping into the dimensional rip herself.

The cold chill of nowhere gripped her for the millisecond it took to cross from one plane to another.

Warmth returned, as did light and sound.

"Where are we?" Dex asked, peeking around.

"I was hoping you knew," she said as she stepped out from behind the trees sitting in large plastic pots. A chlorine smell permeated the air, and everywhere she looked there was white tile.

Dex joined her just as a frosted glass door opened. Valaska immediately held her sword out. However, the two older women, wearing swimsuits and shocked expressions, didn't pose a danger.

Or at least they didn't until they screamed, "Pervert! There's a naked man in the change rooms!"

For some reason, that started a cacophony of screams. Was nudity not allowed wherever they'd found themselves?

"Um, I think we should get out of here," Adexios muttered, hands dropping to cover his package.

"Good plan, but we might perhaps want to garb ourselves on the way out." The less attention they drew, the easier their search, because, upon first glance, she didn't spot the robed figure they were chasing.

As the screeches followed them, along with a few

giggles and whispers of, "Oh my god, did you see the size of him?", Valaska snagged some garments. Adexios practically fell over in his haste to yank the pink shorts over his buttocks. The T-shirt, inscribed with an odd creature sporting horns that said, "Size does matter", covered his chest.

As for Valaska, she snatched a T-shirt from the hands of a young girl gaping at Dex. It proved snug around her chest, but the title across her breasts made her inwardly smile.

Yes, I am a Delicate Freakn' Flower. With thorns. Get in her way and she'd prick a person to death.

Seeing a door, with Member's Area inscribed upon it, Valaska aimed toward it and pushed the bar. She stepped through and blinked as she looked around.

What strange place is this?

Before her sat the oddest contraptions. Metal devices of torture, or so they seemed, given the grimaces on the faces of the humans who used them.

"Have we entered some kind of strange dungeon?" she asked. The groans seemed to lend credence to her query.

"Not quite. I'll be damned."

"You already are," she reminded.

"It seems the rumors are true," Dex muttered.

"What rumors? Do you know what this place is? Where we are?"

"Of course I do. I'm just surprised you don't recognize it. This is a physical fitness center on the mortal plane."

"A what?"

"A gym." At her blank look, he explained further. "Think of it as a training field for exercise."

She grimaced. "A training field? But they are not sparring with blunt swords, leaping over spiked pits, or running away from starving ghouls."

"This is the modern way to build muscle and get great cardio."

"Looks more like it belongs in Lucifer's department for the punishment and correction of evil souls." Although the longer she watched the people grunt and groan and sweat, the more it gave her an urge to pit herself against the metal torture devices.

"Actually, I think some of these contraptions were designed by Hell's engineers."

"Given you seem to recognize this place, care to explain how we got here? I don't see anything to indicate why this place is of import. Why choose this so-called gym to emerge?"

"I'd say there's a few reasons why the thing we're chasing came here," Dex replied, doing his best to peek at every face on every machine, looking for what she couldn't have said. If the person they'd chased had stripped their cloak, they'd never recognize them. "First off, by exiting into a place filled with people, they managed to greatly muddy their trail."

"If they came through here at all."

As soon as she said it, Dex leaned over and snagged some dark fabric, lifting a discarded cloak from the floor. He dangled it in front of her. "Recognize this?"

"At least we know they came through here. And they might come back again."

"Why would they come back? I still don't get what's so special about this place." What she liked about Dex was he didn't lose patience with her questions. Unlike a certain trainer of hers who left a bruise for every W query by a student.

Dex explained. "The amount of intentional suffering in this location has become great enough that it has caused a thin spot between here and Hell. That means it's easier to create a portal from here to back home."

"So they can only conjure one here?"

"Not exactly. It's just easier here. The DMVs are also hotspots, but not as good as they used to be since they automated a lot of their stuff online."

Valaska rubbed her head and leaned on her sword. "Forget I asked. I don't care how this portal got here. Tell me how we find whoever came through."

"I can't." A shrug lifted his shoulder. "Whoever we were chasing got away."

She couldn't help the downturn of her lips. "So there's no one to kill?"

Dex never got a chance to answer, as trouble arrived in the form of a screeching and pointing woman. "There they are. That's the pervert who was ogling me in the women's change room."

Valaska frowned. "Dex was not ogling. Trust me, if he was, I would have plucked his eyes out by now."

A coughing sound from Dex as he said, "Um, I think we should perhaps vacate the premises."

Easier said than done, considering they had to run back through the door into the change room of women, who once again squealed at their appearance.

"Calm down," Valaska snarled as they jogged through. "He's only got eyes for me. And if there's anything perverted happening, it will again, only be with me."

"Are you defending my honor?" Dex asked as they jogged, a trace of amusement in his tone.

"Staking my claim more like," was her pert reply.

They popped behind the potted plants, and she slapped her hand against the wall. It didn't go through.

Dammit. The portal they'd used was gone.

And people were yelling as they chased them.

Dex banged on the wall. "Are you fucking kidding me? Now what are we supposed to do?"

Lifting her blade before she could speak, he growled, "Don't say it. You cannot go on a killing rampage on this plane. Do you know the trouble that would cause?"

Yeah, she knew. God and Lucifer would get into it as the heavenly deity accused Lucifer of cheating to get his souls early before they had a chance to possibly redeem themselves and earn a spot behind his closely guarded gates.

Bullshit really. No one could ever truly atone for all their sins.

That part didn't matter. The rule was, no killing mortals.

She pouted. "Well then, what do you suggest? I don't think these plants will hide us for long."

Fingers spread, he palmed the wall. "I wish that damned portal had lasted a few more minutes."

At his words, a tingling hum filled the air, and her skin pimpled.

Magic. But by who?

Valaska took a step back from the wall that now shimmered.

Not so Dex, who let his fingers dance over the surface. "It's a portal."

"No kidding." She could tell by the way it sizzled with energy. "But where does it go?"

A hand reached out from the portal and grabbed Dex. Valaska only had a moment to latch onto him, too, before they were both pulled into a chilly vortex that spit them out onto a black-and-white checkered floor.

Valaska sprang to her feet, prepared to face the next threat. And, boy, was it a doozy.

"Hi, Mom, I'm home." And while still lying on the floor, Dex said, "Is that cookies I smell?"

Chapter Twenty-one

"You will never be good enough for my son."
Printed on the T-shirt his mom wore.

Springing to his feet, Adexios didn't have to feign pleasure at seeing his mother. Nothing wrong with being a mama's boy, especially since it meant he got to lick the bowl when she baked.

The problem, though, with his mother loving him so much was that she really didn't like other women encroaching on her son's affections.

So it wasn't any wonder that, once his mother released him from a crushing hug, and he stepped back, it was to find Valaska and his mother eyeing each other.

"So you are that Amazon girl Lucifer sent my baby boy off with." Translation. *You're the slut that's been spending time with my son.*

"Yup." *Yup. And he liked it.*

"I don't like you." Trust his mother to not even pretend.

"The feeling is mutual, and I'm sure it will grow stronger over time as we fight for the affection of your son. I will ultimately win. I am, after all, the one screwing him, but I look forward to our future sparring."

Wow, so much to absorb in there. Amidst the subtle taunting and threats, was it him or had Valaska said she was sticking with him?

Judging by his mother's eyes, narrowed with shrewd calculation, yes, she had. "Are you planning to make an honest man of my IO?"

"Mom!" Adexios couldn't help but blush at her direct query—even as he wondered at the answer.

"An honest man in Hell? I would never dare to blaspheme that way." A slow and mischievous grin crossed Valaska's face. "As a matter of fact, it occurred to me that Dex and I should try living in sin for a while."

Yes, that definitely sounded as if she was moving in. Which meant sleeping together. Mental fist pump, revealed only in a push of his glasses atop his nose.

Forget sleeping arrangements. Adexios planned for his funeral when his mother dropped her next bombshell.

"I don't suppose you'd be open to having an out-of-wedlock pregnancy."

"Mom!" Adexios reached a new level of embarrassment.

"What's wrong, baby? You sound upset," his mother said, perusing him with false innocence. "If I'm going to have to tolerate you taking up with a heathen, then I should know what shenanigans you're getting into so I can properly brag to my woman's group. Do you know how jealous Bettina is going to be when she hears about this? You do a mother proud," his mom said, dabbing at the corners of her eyes with her apron.

Anxious to divert the conversation, Adexios asked, "So, where's Dad?"

"At work. Where else? He's sailing the new Wildling Sea."

"Wildling? Is that what they're calling it?" It seemed apt. Sounded like fun, too. Who knew what lay on the other side, but the question was, would the sea remain long enough to find out, or would Lucifer find a way to drain it?

"While you were gallivanting about with your *lady*

friend"—his mother sniffed, looking so delighted at the snub insult—"things have happened. First, the sea levels have stopped rising."

"Probably because we destroyed the portal draining the water from the mortal plane onto this one."

His mother planted her hands on her hips. "Are you getting too big for your britches with me? I was talking, and there you are interrupting me. So rude. I love it!" She cackled, a gleeful, evil sound, and given she was part sorceress, she did it quite chillingly.

"Mom, since you're loving the new me, then love the fact that I am going to ditch you right now and take Valaska back to my place."

"But you haven't had cookies yet." His mother gestured to the oven that glared with baleful red eyes as it heated the dough. "And what about reporting to your father?"

"He can wait."

"This is dereliction of duty," his mother said, whooping. "Merry Christmas to me. Wait until your father hears."

Dad would go off on a fearsome rant of wooden staff and brimstone. It would prove epic, and probably end up on Hell Tube.

Adexios couldn't wait. Just like he couldn't wait to get back to his place. It thankfully wasn't far, and Valaska didn't mind running.

"Impatient?" she teased before she swung up the stairs to his place, giving him a nice view of her ass in those tiny gym shorts she'd grabbed earlier.

He couldn't wait to shed the shorts caught between his cheeks in a major ass-wedgie. Hot pink was not his color. Although he did kind of like the T-shirt. But no self-respecting man would wear just a T-shirt to bed. Not even a geek. It was wrong. Just plain wrong.

And that went for socks too.

Reaching his apartment, Valaska looked at the shut door, pulled a foot back, and kicked.

The door popped open before Adexios could say, "Um, I don't keep it locked."

Mostly because he didn't have that much to steal. He tended to bank the coins he made ferrying souls. He had a fortune sitting in the Goblin's Credit Union.

But Valaska didn't care if he was rich. Or buff.

She just likes me, for me.

Liked with a fierce passion.

Clothing was shredded in their haste to strip.

He'd no sooner let air kiss his naked body than he found himself hitting the bed hard, but not bouncing, as Valaska followed with a pounce.

Their lips met in a clash of teeth and lips. Hot, panting breaths merged as they let loose the passion that constantly simmered between them.

The feel of her naked body against him proved electric. All that skin…

He let his mouth travel the length of her jaw, teasing his way down her neck. He grabbed her by the upper arms, intent on flipping them that he might explore further, but she broke free of his hold.

"Oh, no you don't, Dex. I do believe I lost a wager."

"What wager?"

He sucked in a breath as she reminded him, the fiery feel of her lips nipping and sucking their way down his chest, a tease on the way to her destination.

The headboard provided a perfect place to grip, and he grabbed it just in time, holding on for dear life—and control—as her mouth stopped, poised over the tip of him.

She gave no warning. No foreplay. Nothing.

Just placed her mouth over the head of his cock and swooped down his length, engulfing him in sweet, wet bliss.

"Fuck!" The word expelled from his lips as his hips jerked upwards, ramming his shaft deep into her mouth.

But she took it.

Every inch.

And then she slid back, leaving him wet, aching.

A gasp left him as she flicked the tip with her tongue. He also groaned as she nipped him with her teeth.

Tightly, she suctioned, pulling and sucking and sliding and driving him to the brink.

Then stopping.

He almost cried. He did protest. "Don't stop."

Opening his eyes, he saw her gazing down at him, her eyes bright and her grin wicked. "I've got this covered."

Oh, how she did. She slammed her sex down onto him without mercy. His cock impaled her slick heat, and the headboard creaked as he gripped it with all his strength.

Moist heat pulsed around him. He pulsed within her.

Leaning forward, her lips brushed his as she began to rotate her hips. Grinding herself against him, driving him in so deep.

"Faster," he ordered.

She slowed down, teasing him with a slow pump and swirl.

"Brat," he growled against her lips before nipping the lower one.

"What are you going to do about it?" was her husky taunt back.

"Challenge accepted." Dex flipped them, his powerful arms, and even stronger legs, propelling them so that she lay flat on her back, with him solidly buried in her.

He teased her. Dragging his cock from her sex slowly then ramming it back in. Out, a slow sensual pull. Thrust.

With each stroke, she cried out, and her body tightened, just as he felt his own pleasure coiling.

The exquisite torture saw him pumping faster. Faster. Her fingers clawed at his back. His sac pulled taut. They both reached that climactic edge, and together, they jumped.

He yelled. She yelled. They both came with a fierceness that didn't just shake them both; it collapsed the bed.

The mishap was met with applause. "I dare say, bravo. Points for gusto."

Being caught, ass still clenched, his hips thrust forward in one last push, was only part of the reason for the ruddy heat in Dex's cheeks.

He was more annoyed he didn't get his afterglow. "Do you mind?" Adexios snapped. "I was kind of in the middle of something. Get out."

"While you are definitely in something, you are both done. As to ordering me to leave, I have to say, I appreciate the disrespect. It makes a boss feel good to know that you're working your minions hard enough they're whining."

"I don't whine. I debate."

"Just as bad." Lucifer smiled, yet it never quite reached his eyes on account those were molten swirling pits with fire. "Enough chitchat. I'm a busy devil today what with uprisings to put down, wenches to rescue, and submarines to confiscate. I don't have time to judge a repeat performance. So do us both a favor and just tell me what happened inside the hut."

"I thought you were all seeing."

"That's my brother. Me, I have a life, and I prefer not to spend it in front of the monitoring screens for Hell. A man can only watch so much sin and fornication before he tires of it. I am a man of action." Lucifer posed, a pose somewhat ruined by his mussed hair, unbuttoned jacket, and the hickeys on his neck.

"If I tell you what happened, will you go away?"

"Yes."

"Are you lying?"

"Yes."

"Are you just going to reply yes to anything I say in the hopes of getting caught in a lie?"

Lucifer beamed as he slicked his hair back with his hand. "Yes. Now, if you're done asking questions, it's my turn. What did you find inside the hut?"

Adexios quickly relayed their discovery of the portal devices, and the mysterious figure they'd chased but lost.

"Excellent work." The devil slapped his thigh. "So a mysterious force is conniving against me. They have access to incredible technology and toys that I want!" He breathed a bit of smoke from the nose. "I need to do something about this."

Given the devil would only leave when he was good and ready, Dex didn't see any reason to not tell him his theory. "I have a feeling that volcano island might not have been the only lair."

"You think they have a secret hideaway in Hell? No. No. No. That won't do at all. This is my dirty pit, and I am not sharing." Lucifer growled, pivoting on a bare foot that Adexios just noticed. "I need to mount a hunt."

"If you're going to look anywhere, then start past the shores of the ninth circle and farther even to the edge of the Darkling and Wildling Seas."

"Send some explorers out into uncertainty, adventure, and possible death? What crazy person will volunteer for that?"

"I'm in." Was Adexios as surprised as anyone else that he said it?

Lucifer's brows rose high. "Did you just volunteer to go on a dangerous sea mission?"

"My Dex sure did." Valaska beamed at him, not at all bothered she was lying beneath him naked, the dew of passion still glistening on her skin. "And I'm going with him."

"But how will I explain it to his mother?"

*

A week or so later, on the *S.S. Loveshack*, named to horrify Adexios' mom—and the best Mother's Day present ever, according to her.

Dex saw the eyeball first, blinking at him within the waves. He clutched his oar tight. "Don't you fucking dare," he growled. "This oar is mine!"

The eyeball emerged on a stalk and was soon joined by a half-dozen others. These weren't friends like Sweet. This bunch of sea monsters liked to toy with him.

Probably because he deliberately antagonized them, but with good reason.

The monster feinted at the oar. Adexios managed a quick twist to keep it out of reach. However, the waters were getting rough, so he pulled the paddle out of the water and held it across his chest. "You are not getting it," he said with a huge smirk.

The monster blinked at the taunt. He could see it asking, "*What are you going to do to stop me?*"

Do? Why, sic his brat after them. "Valaska, I need you. There's another one of those monsters trying to steal my paddle."

Some might claim he'd never earn mancard points for calling upon a woman to deal with a misbehaving sea monster. Those idiots had never seen his woman in a bikini. He should elaborate. It was a string bikini, and Valaska rocked it.

From the other end of the long boat, she darted toward him, stripping her short toga robe on the way. Slim, muscular perfection.

Shudder.

He never tired of seeing it.

Because of his need to have her by his side, even at work, the Ferryman's Association had to mint a new title and position—Ferryman's Exalted Huntress. This abuse of power allowed Adexios to bring a woman on board as part of the crew, a move that had many screaming about nepotism—a sin that earned him tickets to the Grand ol' Screamer, currently featuring Hell's most damned singing their repentance.

He couldn't wait until Saturday night's performance. Apparently, the orchestra had been joined by Joey the Flame Lasher. It was said this demonic djinn could whip a line of fire so fine he could create a checkerboard on his victim's skin. But that wasn't all. With the application of some herbs and spice, this top-notch performer also provided an olfactory delight while basting his victim and treating the audience to haunting screams.

But that was much later. Right now, he had a

different show to enjoy.

Pausing for a moment in front of him, Valaska, clad in her sinfully hot bikini, whirled to plant a scorching kiss on his lips. She never failed to take his breath away. Literally sucking it in when she drew his tongue into her mouth for a pleasurable tryst.

Too soon, her lips pulled away, and he opened his eyes to see a bright smile lighting her lips. "I got this, Dex."

With a yell, and one hand gripping a rust-proof trident, she dove into the water, and he sat down to watch the show.

Because watching was all he did these days, that and teaching Sweets new tricks. Right now, his pet sea monster was bobbing alongside his vessel, ready for the apples he tossed her way. He was training her to fling them at targets. The next time the kraken emerged, they'd be ready for them, substituting apples for bombs.

If the massive sea monsters ever returned.

For a while now, he and Valaska, along with other ships manned by intrepid explorers—a title that his mother tended to change to vicious privateer—had sailed these waters. Everything was quiet. Too quiet.

Having been on the water his entire life, Adexios knew when a storm was coming.

I can feel it. The ominous weight of portent. The hush before the boom.

Not finding a trace of the cloak figure that had escaped or, indeed, finding anything at all didn't mean Adexios could shake the nagging suspicion that nothing was over.

I feel like the battle has just begun. A battle he now looked forward to, especially since he'd have Valaska at his side.

Arms flopped over the side of the boat, and his

woman propped her chin on the upraised rim. She eyed him, and he smiled. Leaning back on his pole, he looked down at his bare torso—no more thick robes for him—and said, "See something you like?"

"You know I do."

"Then come and get it."

Her lips widened, and she was about to vault into the boat when a tentacle dared wave from the water.

She eyed it with wavering indecision but turned away from it and made to come to him instead.

Over and over again, it awed him that she chose him.

It was that knowledge that made him stop her from getting on the boat. "I can wait. Go get it, brat."

"Really?"

He nodded. Yes, because the longer he denied himself the pleasure of her, the more intense the rush. So don't mistake his act for kindness. It was total selfishness.

"And this is why I love you!" she yelled with a spurt of glee before diving onto the tentacle and getting her hands around it in a throttling gesture.

The ease with which she said and meant it never failed to swell his heart. Even the ridicule by her tribe mates didn't change her decision to live with him. "Someone needs to protect you from women who would take advantage of you," she'd said.

To which he'd replied, "You can take advantage of me anytime."

She did.

As the days passed, and Adexios sailed the Wildling Sea, he eventually met up with his dad, their ships almost passing in the night. Neither of them had anything to report, but Dex did have a chance to introduce Valaska to his father.

Charon had high praise for her, and yet, for some reason, the compliment turned her pale. "Nice set of bones. Hereditary I hope?"

At least she'd not balked when his mother asked for a pint of her blood for the sausage she was making for Sunday dinner. Quality ingredients for a superb meal. And, yes, attendance was mandatory, even if his mother had to sketch a portal herself.

Speaking of quality, Valaska's head broke the surface, and she sucked in a breath of air.

Holding out the paddle for her to grab, he announced. "I love you. Very much."

"I love you more."

"Do not."

"Do so. And I'll prove it once I get on that boat."

He couldn't reel her in fast enough. But he could love her enough, and even better, she loved him back, too.

And that was all he truly needed—that and his interdimensional fridge in the galley that led to his mom's kitchen.

Epilogue

"You can watch, but keep in mind, I don't share." Lucifer's threat at his engagement dinner speech.

While Gaia's toast went with, "Beyoncé says it best in her song 'Put A Ring On It.' And I'll add, once that ring goes on, ladies and gents, hands off my man. Don't say you weren't warned."

Lucifer and Gaia's engagement party was the event of the season. No, century. Make that the affair that would go down as epic in history—much like Gaia would go down and give him an epic BJ if Lucifer could convince her to crawl under the table.

The bride-to-be wore a lovely flowered gown while Lucifer was stuck in a suit, with a tie! But dammit, if he had to wear a tie, then he was sporting the one covered in deviled duckies, custom made for his lovely fiancée.

How could he resist when he saw their rascally little horns? As for Gaia's reaction upon seeing it?

Grabbing the carefully knotted tie, she yanked Lucifer close and whispered, "You will pay for this, my naughty devil. You. Me. Later. In the garden. The vines will be waiting."

Shudder.

His almost wife threatened the most delicious things. However, she was also a cruel mistress. After her seductive promise, she sashayed off, but not before tossing him a wink over her shoulder and mouthing, "I'm not wearing any panties."

To which his daughter, Muriel, who happened to enter the reception area just as this happened, groaned, "Oh, that's just gross."

"Sex is a wonderful and beautiful thing," Lucifer announced. "How do you think you got here?"

"Immaculate conception," Muriel grumbled.

"Nah. That was my prudish brother who went that route."

"Where is my uncle anyhow?"

"He's sulking because I'm getting married first. Looks like my older brother has lost to me yet again!"

"This is not a competition," Gaia yelled from across the room where she checked on the fire sculpture. It was a re-inaction of the explosion of the volcano at Pompeii.

My fault. Their passion used to know no boundaries back in the day.

"If it was a competition, I'd have won," he muttered.

"Grow up, Dad," Muriel admonished with a kiss to his cheek.

"Never!" he threatened, shaking a fist at her back as she walked away. What a delightful pleasure his daughter had become. Saucy, brave, murderous when threatened, and shacking up with a handful of guys.

If he had the ability to cry, he might have wiped a tear.

Friends and family arrived in singles and pairs and groups for the engagement party and dinner.

All of them came to bask in his triumph. He had netted the most eligible bachelorette in all the galaxy and planes.

Bow to his greatness.

Seriously.

Now. Bow—

Forget it. Your impertinence has earned you a spot in Hell. Remember, I am watching you.

The reception went without a hitch, despite the best attempts by the hired imps to trip waiters and have couples caught in flagrante delicto. But those only resulted in minor flare-ups, nothing worth taping, nothing awesome enough to go viral.

My party is a dud. It would go down in Hell's history as the most boring, uneventful, smoothly run engagement party ever!

He had to do something, something big, but what?

It was during dinnertime that he finally noted a glimmer of hope, as there was a disturbance in the Force. Seriously. Someone had stridden past his castle wards as if they didn't exist.

The sheer gall, and the power that indicated, intrigued him.

Lucifer sat back in his seat, a throne custom-designed from a solid block of obsidian and inlaid with precious gems. He'd had a matching one designed for his wench. A king and his queen holding court.

The lavish feast interested him less than the feel of Gaia's hand inching up his thigh. She did so like to fool around during dinner. The trick was to not lose control.

A trick Lucifer constantly failed, which was why the chef now thought he loved spinach salad with a raspberry vinaigrette. Then again the hollered, "Yes. That's it. Give me more!" might have played a part.

Feigning inattention, when all he wanted to do was look, proved so hard. He could hear the whispers from the crowd.

"Who is that woman?"

"Are those tentacles?"

"Does she have three breasts?" That got him to peek and groan aloud, "Fuck me, the sea hag is back."

"The sea hag is back." The words were repeated in a chain reaction, a chant that accompanied that hag's sinuous glide between the tables, taking a direct path to Lucifer.

Dark hair in shining, dark green, curly waves danced down Ursula's back. The tight mermaid dress left nothing to imagine. It hugged the hourglass curve and displayed the full bosom with its shadowy cleavage tease times two. The obviously custom-made gown hugged the three boobs to perfection.

"You can stop staring anytime," grumbled Gaia with a jab to his ribs.

He clasped her hand in his. "And deny you the enjoyment of jealousy? Even I am not so selfish, wench."

"I am not jealous."

"Such a liar," he murmured. "I love it. I know you hate the fact I slept with her."

"At least you didn't marry her. What is my ex-wife doing here?" groaned Neptune, ducking down on the other side of Lucifer in the hopes Ursula wouldn't see him.

"I don't fucking know, and I don't like it," Lucifer grumbled. "Who had the balls to invite the hag to my party?"

"I thought she was locked in another dimension after her *incident*," Gaia whispered with a gesture, the coo-coo one that involved circling a finger at her temple.

"Yes, I was locked away. Cruelly and unjustly," Ursula said, having reached the head table. She stopped and angled a hip, placing a hand on it, still as voluptuously beautiful as ever, but there was something cold and dark in her eyes.

"You went off your rocker and tried to destroy the world. That kind of thing tends to get noticed," was Lucifer's dry reply.

Ursula took evil to a whole new level, and it seemed her time away had also honed her magic.

Lucifer could feel the power pulsing from her in waves, as if it leaked from her pores. But why had she come? To taunt him with the fact that she'd escaped?

"I was a tad upset after my breakup with that cheating manwhore." Ursula's storm-sea eyes narrowed on Neptune.

The sea god finally found a pair and came out of hiding. Neptune straightened in his seat and stroked his beard. "Maybe I wouldn't have had to step out if you put out more."

An "oooh" went through the room.

Lucifer prepared to erect a force shield to deflect blood.

Nothing happened, nothing except for the tiniest of tics by Ursula's left eye.

"Who truly cares who's at fault?" Ursula coughed in her hand. "You." She smiled. "I am back now, and I didn't come here to rehash the past. I've had time to get over that silliness. I have a much better sex life now." Her laughter emerged high-pitched and ominous. "Today is one of celebration. The Lord of the Pit, the demon who helped lock me away in that dreary dimension with no one to speak to but my constructs and unevolved creatures, is planning to get married. That deserves a gift."

"How about returning the wilds back the way they were?" Lucifer missed the weed he smoked for relaxation that used to come out of the swamps.

With a melodrama Lucifer remembered well, Ursula flung her head back and placed a hand upon her temple. "Trying to kick me out of my new home already? And after all the time and effort I spent creating it?" She snorted and tilted her head to face him. Ursula's swirling eyes took on the color of an arctic sea, cold and uncompromising. "Not happening. I am back, bitches, and I am here to stay. And in a gesture of goodwill and a sincere wish to make things work, I want to give you the kiss of peace."

Peace offering, no war? No bloody battles or catfights?

Worst party evah!

Curvy red lips puckered for a kiss. As if Lucifer was insane enough to kiss another woman in front of his fiancée. Gaia could hold a grudge. He pulled back. "Couldn't we just shake?"

"In order to make the peace between us binding, it requires something a little more *intimate*."

Gaia shoved at him. "Don't be such an imp. It's just a kiss. Take it like a demon and get this over with."

"But you told me I wasn't allowed to touch anyone else. You threatened"—Lucifer lowered his voice—"my manparts if I did."

"You still aren't, except for this one case. Now pucker up, buttercup, and take your kiss like a big boy."

"Fine. But I won't like it."

Lucifer leaned forward and presented his mouth. He closed his eyes, too, as Ursula pressed in close. Closer.

Don't like it. Don't like it. No matter what Gaia said, Lucifer knew he'd be in big trouble if he did.

Thankfully, Lucifer barely felt the touch of Ursula's lips. Just a tiny electrical shock. The teensiest of zaps.

The entire assembly held its breath. You could have heard a fairy let out gas.

And…Lucifer felt nothing. No urge at all to toss this past sex partner and ex-wife of a friend—which made sex with her totally taboo—onto a table and have his way.

As Ursula pulled back and he opened his eyes, a relieved sigh went through the room.

A room full of the people he loved most in all of Hell. The world. Everywhere.

As Lucifer's gaze bounced around from face to face, he noted the people he'd gotten to know over the years, some of whom he'd personally mentored—and, according to a few, traumatized. He saw many minions whom he'd forged in the fires of hell and made stronger.

To see so many of them here, supporting him, made his heart swell, and he couldn't help but exclaim. "I love you! Each and every one of you. Group hug!"

The devil held out his arms, but no one moved. He grinned wider. "Come on. Don't be shy. Let's share the love."

"Um, Luc, are you feeling all right?" Gaia asked, placing her hand lightly on his arm.

He whirled and grasped her hand, holding it tenderly. "Never better, my beautiful fiancée. Have I told you how much I love you? And how excited I am that we're getting married and spending the rest of our lives together? Ooh. Do you know what would make our wedding day even better?" he gushed.

"What?"

"Abstaining from intimate acts until the big day."

"What!"

"Think of it as me showing my respect and affection for you. My beloved." Lucifer couldn't help but beam, overcome with emotion.

More than a few people gagged.

"Luc, are you screwing with me?" Gaia peered at him with worry.

"Never, my gentle dove." He would never do anything so crude to his delicate lady.

Gaia whirled away from him, seeming upset for some reason. Perhaps he should offer to fetch her a soothing tea and give her a nice foot massage.

Before he could ask her to sit, Gaia braced her hands on her hips and barked, "Get your fat ass back here, you psycho, dimension-escaping hussy. What did you do to Lucifer?"

Whirling, Ursula clutched at a breast and widened her eyes dramatically. "What did I do? Why only what I said I would. I gave Lucifer the gift of peace. Oh, and it might have had a smidgen of love and respect in there. Look at him. He's a changed man already." Ursula laughed, the slow, rolling chuckle of pure evil. "Muahahaha. Muahahahaha."

"Change him back," Gaia said in a low growl.

"Um, no. Like I said, the bitch is back, and I am promising some trouble. Enjoy your pussy of a boyfriend!" With a snap of her fingers, and a poof of smoke, Ursula disappeared from sight.

But she wasn't forgotten.

"Wasn't that just lovely of her to pop in like that?" Lucifer said with his brightest smile. "Now who wants some cake? Don't forget to say please."

The End.

Never…

Stay tuned for the next story in Hell by either signing up for Eve's newsletter, keeping an eye on her website, or stalking her on Facebook.

Facebook: http://bit.ly/faceevel

Website: http://www.EveLanglais.com
Newsletter: http://evelanglais.com/newrelease

Made in the USA
Charleston, SC
17 October 2015